'Endlessly funny, endlessly inventive – a bold and stylish novel that slipped down and burned like a shot of something lovely'

Rebecca Wait, author of *I'm Sorry You Feel That Way*

'*The Happy Couple* is a dazzling follow-up to *Exciting Times*. Dolan spins her magic again with humour and insight and the sharpest of prose. Not a word out of place'

Katherine Heiny, author of *Standard Deviation* and *Early Morning Riser*

'We predict a hit' *The Times*

the happy couple

Naoise Dolan

WEIDENFELD & NICOLSON

First published in Great Britain in 2023 by Weidenfeld & Nicolson,
an imprint of The Orion Publishing Group Ltd
Carmelite House, 50 Victoria Embankment
London EC4Y 0DZ

An Hachette UK Company

5 7 9 10 8 6

A CIP catalogue record for this book is
available from the British Library.

ISBN (Hardback) 9781474613491
ISBN (Export Trade Paperback) 9781474613507
ISBN (eBook) 9781474613521
ISBN (Audio) 9781474613538

Typeset by Input Data Services Ltd, Bridgwater, Somerset

Printed in Great Britain by Clays Ltd, Elcograf, S.p.A.

MIX
Paper from
responsible sources
FSC® C104740

www.weidenfeldandnicolson.co.uk
www.orionbooks.co.uk

For John and the McNallys

Contents

PART I

The Bride

I

They got engaged like this.

In Dublin they went to a house party, then walked home along cobblestoned lanes. Celine was twenty-six and Luke was twenty-eight. He was tall and lean and dark-haired, and wore a half-tucked pale blue shirt. She was tastefully ugly: square face, flat black sandals. Although the night was warm, she had gloves on.

Both were fast talkers, but his tone was steady while her own had more vigour. They discussed two of the guests who'd broken up.

'I don't think they spoke to each other all night,' Celine said.

'Honestly they should have ended it sooner,' Luke replied.

'How so?'

'I mean, break-ups always suck. But they suck a lot less if you end it while you still like each other.'

They strolled left onto a street of terraces. Celine turned the key in their red panelled front door, and together they clambered up the rickety communal stairs. Their two-room flat was in No. 23, a subdivided Georgian townhouse.

The boiler kept breaking, the main local amenity was the man who sold weed from his Nissan, and rent was two thousand euro per month.

When they'd moved in last year, the landlord had warned them: 'This ain't The Ritz, lads.' Celine faced little difficulty remembering this fact. Their hallway had a coconut mat and brass shoe rack: here you trapped dirt at the entrance, while The Ritz allowed dirt to travel anywhere so long as it paid. Bedroom and bathroom were plain and poky, and unfortunately weren't The Ritz. The living area contained Celine's piano and a green-and-yellow kitchenette. There was nowhere to put a table. This wasn't, please note, The Ritz; so they ate on the couch.

At the bathroom sink, Celine removed her black leather gloves and rubbed in hand cream. She was a professional pianist, and moisturised only at night to avoid smearing lotion on the keys.

Then she wiped her hands with a tissue and joined Luke in bed. On contact with his body, she let out an Oh, as if him lying there was a surprise.

She resumed the topic from earlier.

'No one ends a relationship while they still like the other person,' she said. 'You think, okay, it's bad, but it's about to get good again. Then it keeps being bad till it's over.'

'Decide up front,' Luke said. 'What's the worst thing they could do where you'd still like them, but only just. That's your limit, and if they do it then leave. Or you could use – you know those feedback forms?'

'Circle 10 for adore new microwave, or circle 0 for dislike new microwave and wish it ill?'

'Yeah.'

'I'm not sure that works for gauging if you're happy.'

4

'Maybe not,' Luke said.

Celine held back the words: Are you happy, though?

They did not, as a rule, 'share feelings'. Celine's family had never taught her how. To see the tint of your internal mood ring as warranting disclosure, and to expect a rapt audience – no, no. Have you met Irish people? But they'd been together for three years, and Celine measured their relationship in clutter. Luke's battered paperbacks lined the windowsills; he'd procured a coffee grinder and half a cat. The other half was hers, and the asset would be difficult to divide, so hopefully they were in it for the long haul.

Celine turned off the bedside lamp. 'So what's your limit? In theory.'

'I mean, it sounds old-fashioned.' Luke paused, as if waiting for her to pull out the rest of his words from him. 'But if I thought we'd never get married. Or that level of commitment. If I knew that wasn't going to happen, then – yeah. In theory.'

'When you say it won't happen, who's decided?'

'I didn't say that.'

'If you're a mindreader, you know that's going to cause way more problems than it solves.'

'I didn't say it won't . . .' Luke trailed off. 'I mean, but it won't, though. Marriage will never happen between us. And that's not a problem necessarily. It would be silly to stop when it's going well. But we're not going to end up together.'

A pause, for which Celine felt responsible. The cat mewed from the next room.

Celine said at last: 'If you really think that, we should break up right now.'

No response from Luke.

She added: 'By your own criteria.'

Silence.

'But,' Celine said, 'sometimes you say things because you want me to contradict you. And it's fine if you don't and you want me to agree.'

Still no answer.

'Tell me what to say,' she said.

'Say what you want.'

'I guess one of us has to. Like − I think back a lot to when you said you didn't want a relationship. And I said, eventually I want one with someone, but not a guy I've just met, so for now we're good. Then later I said if you still didn't want anything serious, we should stop. And you said you'd changed your mind. Sometimes I think you'd always wanted to be with me. You just couldn't acknowledge it until I did.'

Another pause.

'If I need to say things aloud before you'll even say them in your head,' Celine said, 'then that's not my favourite quality of yours. It's not an aspect I'd bring to a desert island if I could only take three. But I'd still have a hard time choosing. Actually, I'd find it impossible, picking only three things. Probably I love all of you. And I think for me that means I want to be with you forever.'

Then Luke asked.

2

Everyone else wanted the wedding in Dublin, but Aunt Maggy preferred London, so London it would be.

Celine was from Dublin and had never lived elsewhere. Luke had grown up in London, but his parents were Irish and he'd moved back to the old country three years ago.

Dublin seemed obvious.

Celine wrote 'DUBLIN' in her little black book.

They still wound up setting the ceremony in London.

★ ★ ★

'You use the engagement party to sort the guest list,' Aunt Maggy told Celine from her London landline. 'Tell me if there's racket. I'm dusting the birds.' The birds were Maggy's Waterford Crystal swans, plus a few outliers: hawk, eagle, pigeon. Uncle Grellan had once made the mistake of buying Maggy a Tipperary sparrow. The species Maggy could accept, but it had to be Waterford. Give money to Tipperary? Would she fuck.

Maggy had married Celine's Uncle Grellan when they were young London Irish immigrants in the eighties. They had no children of their own, so Maggy was forever bothering her two nieces. Having formed a remark, she was powerless but to pass it, and she'd never met business that she couldn't make her own.

Admittedly she was not one of the people getting married. But she had resources.

Through the success of their plumbing firm, Uncle Grellan and Aunt Maggy had bought a massive house in north London. Meanwhile, Celine and Luke's Dublin square footage was a luxurious 80 per cent of the legal minimum.

Maggy's opening gambit: 'We'll host the engagement party.'

Fair enough. She had the will; she had the space.

In this way Maggy got her inch. Next came the mile.

'I'd wonder your mother never taught you about engagement parties,' Maggy continued to Celine on the phone. 'But she was busy. Off being a doctor and divorcing your father. Well, miss, here's the score. You see who turns up for the engagement party, and then you know how many'll be at the wedding.'

'Fine,' Celine said. She was violently allergic to two things: logistics, communications.

'Except –' Maggy said. 'No matter. A shame, but sure look.'

This was when Celine first sensed she was being had. She didn't know how, or over what, but Maggy used a special voice for what she viewed as her master manipulation.

'If you've the engagement party in a different country to the wedding,' Maggy said, 'then you've no way of telling who'll come. And it's a year away, the wedding. Who knows where any of us will be? Mallorca, maybe, or Meath. But listen, there's ways of predicting. If the party's in London this June, and the wedding's in London next June –'

You didn't interrupt Aunt Maggy's efforts to persuade. She'd feel robbed, even cuckolded.

★ ★ ★

When Luke got home that night to No. 23, Celine told him: 'I've done a terrible thing.'

'Honestly so have I,' Luke said.

Celine patted the cushion and Luke joined her on the couch.

Stirred by Luke's arrival, their blue-eyed Siamese cat hopped onto the piano and prowled across the lid. They'd named her Madame Esmeralda after the composer Franz Liszt's pet. ('Just some of the pussy in Liszt's life,' Celine's sister Phoebe had remarked.) Although Madame Esmeralda hated other felines, she cherished her humans for their opposable thumbs. They were lousy gymnasts and alarmingly hairless, but they opened her chicken cans, and that was not nothing.

It was getting dark. Celine stood up and closed the curtains, then returned to the sofa and stretched her feet across to Luke.

He stroked her ankle, and said: 'I got our country manager to say we're "standing athwart the market".'

Luke was a communications strategist at a multinational tech firm that had bought up Dublin's docklands for its headquarters. He took a morbid interest in company lingo. Initially he'd restricted himself to writing it all down, but soon he was making up his own. Office jargon was weirdly nautical – 'onboarding', 'run a tight ship' – so he drew from there, and waited to see which words spread.

'What's "stand athwart the market"?' Celine asked Luke.

'We're still deciding,' he said. 'I wanted to imply we're on the sidelines. But my boss heard the "thwart" in "athwart" and took it to mean outfoxing our many foes.'

'You're much misunderstood. But my thing's worse.'

9

She told him.

He said nothing for a while. Then: 'We can work with that.'

'Are you sure?' Celine said. 'I know you wanted the wedding in Dublin.'

'I mean, if London makes you happy,' Luke said.

'It'll make Aunt Maggy happy,' Celine said. 'And that'll make Uncle Grellan happy, which will make my mother happy, and they're the people I'm getting married for. Besides you. And one other, I guess.'

'Yourself?'

'The cat.'

As if on cue, Madame Esmeralda sunk her teeth into a mouse toy, carried it from the windowsill and dropped it on the couch. Luke petted the side of her face. 'You're too kind,' he said. 'Merci, Madame, for zis gift.'

'She thinks you can't feed yourself,' Celine said. 'Thank God she's not an outdoor cat or it'd be rabbit heads. But there's something else I meant to say.'

'You're full of surprises.'

'This one's not my fault,' Celine said. 'Nor was the other, I'll stress. You try arguing with middle-aged Irish women.'

'I'll have the privilege in fourteen years.'

'I will not be middle-aged in fourteen years.'

'You're twenty-six,' Luke said. 'Middle-aged starts at forty.'

'You're older.'

'True. There'll be a two-year interval where you argue with a middle-aged spouse and I don't.'

'But the second thing,' Celine said. 'We have to invite Maria.'

This time Luke was speechless.

3

Six years ago, Celine thought Maria was the greatest love she'd ever know.

★ ★ ★

'This won't end well,' Maria said.

It was spring. They sat by Dublin's canal in Portobello drinking canned cocktails. Maria had a confident stride, dark lipstick and a large collection of men's shirts. They were both twenty and halfway through their bachelor degrees at the Royal Irish Academy of Music. Across their cohort, they were the two best keyboard students.

Maria put her hand on Celine's. 'I'm Salieri,' she said. 'And you're Mozart. And we're rival composers and I'm out to beat you, but you're just having fun. So I murder you.'

Celine looked at their hands. 'No murder, please.'

Maria said: 'I'll try.'

'To kill me?'

'To be with you.'

★ ★ ★

The August after their final exams, they started renting an apartment even tinier than the one Celine would eventually share with Luke.

From there, Celine and Maria began their careers as professional pianists. Celine's dream was to earn a living through concerts alone. Maria craved prizes and La Scala and record deals. Back in reality, they both took pupils to pay the bills.

One of their conservatoire teachers had privately told Celine that she was the better artist and Maria the better performer. Maria's candid, effusive manner could make any audience feel things. Celine's style was foxier, full of hints, allusions, jokes. Musicians loved Celine; everyone loved Maria. Celine didn't mind. The world had room for both of them. But Maria seemed unable to shake her own suspicion that being popular made her worse – and/or that Celine must secretly think so.

At every milestone, Maria got there first. Then Celine caught up, and Maria felt outshone.

Maria's reaction:

1. Maria isn't unambiguously happy for Celine, which makes Maria a bad girlfriend.

2. Okay, Celine didn't say Maria was a bad girlfriend, but Celine is thinking it. Maria can tell.

3. Maria wonders if Celine can actually have been unambiguously happy when Maria achieved it first. If so, then Celine is a better person – and 'better than Maria' is, we've established, vexed emotional territory.

4. If Celine was only pretending to be gracious, then Maria wants her to know there's space to say that. But also, Celine managed to hide her resentment

when Maria would never be able to, which makes Celine better at stoicism. And fine, best her at that, heap the betterment, what indeed is Maria but chopped liver, be better than Maria in every way why don't you.

They'd both grown up believing you had to dominate others to get ahead. But they'd responded differently. Maria needed to win. Celine thought: Okay, I will simply not dominate others and not get ahead.

It wasn't that Celine was lazy. She played for playing's sake.

Once she'd begun learning a new piece, she gave herself over. She started with the hardest passages, so that by the end they'd be the bars she played for fun. There was only time to physically practice five hours a day – anyway, more than that was asking for tendonitis – but she never stopped mentally rehearsing. A black-and-white keyboard inhabited her brain. She played it while scrubbing dishes, queuing in Lidl, and riding the bus to students' homes. Her cerebrum's running score left no energy to speak – not even to Maria.

For Celine, this was bliss.

★ ★ ★

'You can't say you don't want to talk to me and not say sorry at all,' Maria said in the entrance hall after Celine had emerged from a week-long Liszt coma. 'Could you not just apologise?'

'But I'm not sorry.' Celine placed her umbrella on the radiator. It was September and it rained every day. 'Or else I wouldn't do it.'

'I need to know you regret hurting me.'

'But I don't regret it or I wouldn't –'

Et cetera.

The disagreement was not whether Celine should sometimes ignore Maria. They were both fine with that. Maria was less available to Celine day-by-day than Celine was to Maria, since Maria's focus was more evenly spread.

The problem was that Maria could apologise when neither felt she'd actually done anything wrong. Celine couldn't.

'It's lying,' Celine said, 'and lying is stressful.'

'But it's not lying.' Maria put her own umbrella next to Celine's. 'Even though you did the right thing, you're still sorry for how it made me feel.'

'That's not what sorry means.' Celine was crying now. 'Sorry is when there was unfairness.'

They had this fight roughly once a month for three years.

★ ★ ★

But when it was good, it was the best.

Sex, for instance.

Celine had long seen orgasm as physically beyond her. She'd never climb Everest; she'd never kayak; she'd never come.

Her male partners had sportingly borne this limitation.

(At least, they had eventually, after first insisting that every other woman they'd been with had managed. Here Celine's obliviousness became an accidental power move. She didn't have the confidence to fake it, not after hearing how many real ones they'd definitely seen. No way could she fool these stallions.)

The sex toy argument was another of Celine and Maria's staples.

'It'd take me out of the moment,' Celine said one night in October.

'Okay,' Maria said, 'but it takes me out of the moment when I'm the only one who comes. Can you at least try a vibrator on your own?'

'It won't work. I've tried everything.'

'Except the thing I'm suggesting.'

'It won't work.'

★ ★ ★

Then, after two years of dating and four months of living together, they went to Japan. It was mid-December. Celine was playing at a competition in Tokyo. When the judges announced that Celine had finished third, Maria muttered to Celine that the winner had been 'lethally inoffensive'. Celine replied: 'Third is good. Stop ruining third for me.'

That night they returned to the hotel room. The carpet was thick between Celine's toes, and Maria's perfume smelled of lilies and wood.

'I've an early Christmas present for you,' Maria said.

It appeared to be a mint green stress ball in a little glass case. Celine took it out, and squished it in her hand. 'Cute,' she said. 'Thank you. That's really – oh.'

It buzzed.

'If it doesn't work, we'll try a Swedish one,' Maria said. 'The Swedes rule on function, but it's the Japanese for design.'

'I don't know,' Celine said. 'If I try it and I still can't come, then I'll have to accept I'm broken.'

'I can't believe I'm the first partner to give you a vibrator,' Maria said. 'Men are Luddites. Just smashing up the hated machine that's stolen a man's job. And at least the Luddites were good. Their weaving worked. It just wasn't

15

fast. In this case, a whole lot of cloth was never happening in the first place.'

'Fine,' Celine said. 'Let's try.'

★ ★ ★

Two minutes.

It took two minutes.

She could forgive men everything but this.

★ ★ ★

If their relationship had consisted solely of sex, Celine would have married Maria.

The problem was everything else.

Besides Maria's professional envy, there were also her vendettas. She spilled much wine on their mottled carpet while ranting about how everyone was obsessed with her, but also neglected her, but also wanted to get with her, but also wanted her dead.

Celine could participate. In fact, she was better on a craft level. None of it held emotional valence for her, so she had the mental clarity to compose snider quips than Maria's piqued incoherence could match. But Maria's grudges kept changing. There were different enemies each week, and tiers within the category. This part Celine couldn't assess, since it required not analysis (her sharpest sword) but perception (her armorial chink). She did the thing she was good at – arranged words to form bitch-slap – then found she had slapped too hard or slapped the wrong bitch.

'I was messaging Jack,' Maria said one summer afternoon as they walked through the tightly packed stalls of George's Street Arcade. 'And I'm messaging Ró too, and Ró says she's also messaging Jack and he's not replying at all. Like, Jack. Ró's your girlfriend. Do Ró first.'

16

Celine said: 'He's hoping she'll grow into you if he leaves her fallow.'

And that crossed the limit. Jack and Ró were in their circle, at a distance where you could be kind of mean but not fully.

Maria's social awareness was peripheral and constant, while Celine only noticed when actively focusing; and then she saw too much. Maria could hint that Jack was secretly – who wasn't? – an undying Mariast. But Celine thought it all the way through, and verbalised the endpoint. Privately, Celine believed Jack did prefer Ró and just replied faster to people who gave him anxiety, e.g. by slagging him off behind his back. For someone sick of her countless alleged admirers, Maria sure didn't tire of bringing them up. And why always to Celine? If Maria needed male validation, maybe someone else could help – a man, say.

Celine never said any of this to Maria. She was too afraid of how Maria might spin it to someone else.

★ ★ ★

They'd been together for nearly three years when Celine played a Brahms concerto with an orchestra in Madrid. While Celine sat in the dressing room, Maria rang.

Celine curled and uncurled her fingers. The thumbs clicked. Had she practiced too hard?

'Is it tomorrow you're back?' Maria said on the phone.

'Sorry,' Celine said. She stretched her fingers again. 'I forgot to tell you – they added a couple of nights in Seville.'

Maria said: 'I can't believe they're making you stay.'

'They're not making me. They offered and I said yes.'

'You know I'm in Prague tomorrow?'

'Yes,' Celine said. 'Text me how you get on.'

'I'll be gone all week.'

'You said.'

'Which adds up to a month apart.'

Oh.

Maria expected Celine to guess how she felt, and took it as wilful neglect when Celine failed. Was it this hard for everyone?

'I'm sorry,' Celine said.

'You don't care about me,' Maria said. 'I put all the work in.'

Celine herself only made such statements if she considered them beyond reasonable dispute. But Maria played opposites. She said one thing and your job was to contradict. 'You don't care about me' meant 'Tell me you care', and 'I put all the work in' meant 'Tell me you're still committed'.

With Luke, Celine would eventually learn the rules of this game. In the moment, though, Celine assumed she'd received a verdict that she had to accept. Maria was better at people, and Maria knew how Maria felt.

'I'm sorry, Maria,' Celine said. 'I'm sorry for all that.'

'I'm done.'

After years together, they needed strenuous effort to communicate. Each felt she made herself unhappy for the other. The relationship was always going to end.

But the break-up still hurt like hell.

★ ★ ★

After they parted, Celine could still make herself sit down and play piano. But throughout the rest of the day, the keyboard in her head disappeared. Someone had closed the lid. She lumbered along Dublin's rainy streets; each step was slower without her internal soundtrack. In her new single bedroom she listened to late Beethoven, all-career-stages

Beyoncé, and – who among the newly dumped hasn't? – 'I Will Survive'.

Her pupils kept her busy. Throughout that winter and into the new year, Celine thought more and more about her students' sightreading and their *Für Elise*, and less and less about how cold she felt. She kept her eyes on their little hands and told them not to rush.

Key by key, her inner piano returned.

One spring day, while she waited at the bus stop, Taylor Swift's 'I Forgot That You Existed' came up on shuffle. Celine wasn't quite there yet – but then, nor was Taylor, or she wouldn't have written the song. The cultural ephemera we use to get over our exes is reliant on the labour of those who weren't over theirs.

Celine didn't date again until the summer. She knew she'd be lost for a time – and she was, until she met Luke.

4

'Explain to me once more,' Luke said in the sitting room at No. 23, 'I mean explain to me – like I'm a child – why we need to invite Maria to our engagement party.'

The cat jumped onto the windowsill and kneaded Luke's books as if braiding bread. She worked unaware of her owner's gaze, absorbed as she was by her craft. Madame Esmeralda was Celine's familiar in this respect: she never let a small thing like human interaction derail her creative pursuits.

Celine turned her head back to Luke. 'Aunt Maggy's one kind of middle-aged Irish woman. She's military efficiency. She's Prussia. But my mother's more into soft power, and Maria's parents live on her road.'

'Are we inviting everyone on your mother's road?' Luke said.

'There's neighbours and there's neighbours. The Burkes are neighbours.'

'Right. We need to invite your bad ex because these neighbours aren't just neighbours, but neighbours.'

'She's not a bad ex,' Celine said. 'She's just an ex. And she won't come.'

'Then why invite her?'

'We can't invite the Burkes and not Maria,' Celine said. 'The Burkes won't come either, but they'd mind not being asked.'

'This isn't soft power. This is a national phobia of the word "no".'

'I'm telling you, Maria won't come.'

5

Of course Maria came.

6

'I didn't think you'd come,' Celine said, and made to hug just as Maria went for a cheek kiss.

'Are we hugging?' Maria said. She withdrew the kiss.

It was the first time they'd seen each other in months. Their last brief encounter had been at a friend's New Year's drinks, which Celine had attended with Luke.

'Were you in London anyway?' Celine said.

'I've moved here,' Maria said. 'Where's Luke?'

★ ★ ★

Uncle Grellan's Hampstead house was called The Birches. It had three storeys, a red-brick facade and two white pillars.

In the entrance hall was a spiral staircase. Floor-to-ceiling shelves featured no books, no plants, and many Waterford swans.

Double doors opened to the reception rooms. On the dining table were chopping boards with antipasti that Aunt Maggy had deemed 'continental': salami, olives, and Tesco Biscuits for Cheese. She'd considered splashing out on Tesco Finest Assorted, but crackers were crackers, and facts were facts.

Tastes as static as Aunt Maggy's will occasionally find that fashion has revolved to meet them. Maggy despised carpet, and had weathered the wall-to-wall decades in the knowledge her time would come. Her pride and joy, the polished maple floors, once more announced: rich people live here. She was presently wrong on her other love, patterns. Her floral velvet curtains were not in vogue. But stay standing where you are – and vogue, like Fedex, will call again.

★ ★ ★

'Luke's somewhere,' Celine told Maria. 'There are a few others you'd know. Tanja, Ró, Jack, Gráinne –'

She and Maria stood by the staircase. She pointed to their old conservatoire friends, who sat on two chaise longues outside the dining room.

'– and Phoebe's in the garden, badgering people for smokes.'

Celine could see her twenty-two-year-old sister through the back window. Pink eyeshadow, white chunky sneakers, chatting to two of their cousins. She expressed herself with her usual tragicomic range of gestures, and was most likely being rude about Luke. Phoebe had never taken to him. She was difficult like that.

The girls' father wasn't there. He was a cautious, aloof man, a doctor like their mother. Until he left, he'd helped Celine with every Sunday crossword. She was eleven then, and had never attempted one since, but she pretended to her father she'd kept the habit up. She couldn't tell him it had never been about the puzzles.

Luke's father hadn't come, either. As far as Celine knew, he was a failed actor who'd given Luke his breezy voice and not much else.

'But where's Luke?' Maria asked again. 'I was hoping for a heart-to-heart.'

24

'You'd need to have one for that to work,' Celine said. They both laughed.

'You're talking to me,' Maria said. 'Out of everyone you could be talking to. So I can't be that bad.'

'Brava,' Celine said. 'You've won the engagement party.'

'I'm in the lead. I still need to find Luke. You know, I've barely met him.'

'What's your impression so far?'

Maria considered. 'Modestly attractive and doesn't say much. Used to be a fuckboy but always knew he'd settle down. That's the thing about fuckboys. They're not afraid. They know someone will have them when they're ready.'

'I'm always amazed,' Celine said, 'how well you understand people you hardly know.'

'Am I wrong?'

'You're never wrong, Maria. That's for the modestly attractive.'

They couldn't have teased each other with their old brutality if they'd met on the street. But parties were different. Normal life took a pause.

Parties also forced decisions. Celine remembered the good times with Maria, but the bad was surfacing too. In a room with both Maria and Luke, she'd talk to Luke.

Where had he gone?

Celine had last seen Luke around 8 p.m., when she'd been looking for her camera. She still hadn't found it, but Maggy's photographer cousin had stepped in.

That was the camera solved. The Luke question remained open.

Celine messaged him. He didn't reply.

He tended to float off, and he'd never been much of a

texter. She knew that, and for the most part she accepted it. But did he have to do it tonight?

Where was he?

7

Ever since her conservatoire days, Celine had experienced grave doubts when she compared her own life to Franz Liszt's. The Hungarian composer had many mistresses, one of whom wrote a scandalous novel about him, and he did just about everything you can do and not die. Then he died, fine, but his music — only where did he find the time? Celine spent five of her waking hours on piano practice, nine on whatever paid the bills, and the last two on getting clean and fed.

Besides Luke and her pupils, Celine spoke to no one most days. She was generally a hermit, and waited for the next party to be a person again.

★ ★ ★

One such party was where Celine had first met Luke three years ago.

It was a hot day in early July. She was in someone's dingy kitchen. On the countertop a bronze Bluetooth radio played Kate Bush's 'Running Up That Hill'. C minor, key of angst: fifteen-year-old Felix Mendelssohn's first symphony, Walter Page's 'Blue Devil Blues', Bon Jovi's 'It's My Life'. And 'Blame It on the Boogie', but don't split hairs.

Many of Kate Bush's lines landed on the minor seventh, a note that's meant to go somewhere, only it didn't. And that was why Celine had learned theory to predict what was coming, to feel a shiver when deprived. 'You need to know the rules before you break them' – no, you don't, but knowing them deepens the impact when they're broken. To a trained ear, scales can tease. A seventh is a hand on your thigh.

A man by the door met her eye. 'I heard something about – you lost your vodka.'

Ah, yes. Celine had been telling her friends in the kitchen before Kate Bush distracted her.

The man was handsome, so she accepted a shot of his Smirnoff. He mixed it with soda and handed her the plastic cup.

His name was Luke. He spoke in a strangely confident mumble, letting words fall with the profligate spirit of one who could always make more. Later Celine would realise he only enjoyed talking one-on-one, and was quiet in groups; but that first night, with her, he said a lot. His accent was southern English and something else.

'Are you liking Ireland?' Celine said.

It transpired the something else was Dublin. He'd grown up in London, but he picked up a bit of whatever he was around. Not always; only when he on some level wanted to; he didn't sound San Franciscan when his tech firm flew him to the Bay – but anyway.

'By the way,' Luke added, 'can I ask why you're wearing gloves?'

Celine held up her palms. 'I play piano and I'm neurotic about my hands. Slip knife, lose a finger. Spill kettle, lose a finger. Septic papercut –'

Then Luke asked what she was doing that weekend.

At the time she'd thought nothing of that sequence. Later, Luke told her his invitation was in response to the gloves. 'I'd never met someone so focused on one thing,' he'd said. 'I thought, let's figure her out.'

★ ★ ★

On their first date, they went to a dimly lit wine bar and argued about talent.

Celine said it didn't exist.

'I probably shouldn't tell you this,' Luke replied, 'but I found a video of you playing *Gaspard de la nuit*. You can't tell me anyone can do that.'

'If they go through the stages –' Celine said.

'You go through the stages by having talent.'

'No, you go through the stages by going through the stages.'

'Then why doesn't everyone?' Luke said. 'If it's easy to play like you –'

'I didn't say it was easy. I said anyone can do it. It's not easy to count to a million, but you can.'

'Is piano really that tedious?'

'Sometimes,' Celine said. 'But I love it, even when I hate it.'

'Honestly that's what I mean by talent,' Luke said. 'Everyone wants applause, but not everyone wants the process from start to end. I reckon I define talent as having some element inside you that you didn't put there yourself. And you can't just decide to love piano. So by talent, I mean – yeah, love.'

'Actually I don't even want applause,' Celine said. 'It's like – I already got the good bit. I got to play.'

'Interesting,' Luke said.

Celine waited for the 'buts': but my process is different, but I need an audience, but does that mean you're the real artist and I'm a populist hack?

That was Maria, though – not Luke.

To Maria, Celine had been a mirror. Luke looked at Celine without needing to see himself.

8

Trust Archie to arrive at the engagement party near midnight.

Celine saw him approach from the drawing room window. She rushed to let him in before Aunt Maggy could. Archie was Luke's best friend so Celine had to tolerate him, but cokehead lawyers were a virus best contained.

Archie stood in the doorway, a champagne bottle in each hand; he must have rung the bell with his elbow. He wore a black cashmere coat and a diamond-patterned scarf. 'Mam'selle Dion,' he said, and wetly smooched Celine's cheeks. 'Ravishing percussionist. Or string? How do pianos work?'

Definitely on coke.

'Good of you to come.' Celine led him in. 'Let's get these in the fridge' – since the champagne was for Luke, who'd disappeared from the party.

He still hadn't replied to Celine's text.

The narrow kitchen staircase was at the back of the entrance hall. Celine showed the way. 'I think Luke's taking a work call,' she improvised as Archie followed her down the steps. 'But I'm glad you came.'

When Celine was actually glad someone came, she was too busy enjoying their company to register such a mundane thought.

'A work call at his engagement party.' Archie whistled. 'The boy's in demand.'

Perhaps some other class of stimulant.

Archie made room in the fridge for the champagne bottles with the cheetah's agility he applied to one task at a time. Then he straightened up and said solemnly: 'Between us, I'm already tight. Locked, as Hibernians phrase it. I've consumed rather a lot of alcohol, and am drunk.'

Luke often said that Celine and Archie 'should' be great pals. She still wasn't sure if it was a prediction or a decree.

'Everyone's drunk,' Celine told Archie. 'Vivian's here, by the way, and Shawn.'

Vivian and Shawn were the friends Luke and Archie had lived with in London after university. Luke had dated both Vivian and Archie when they were all Oxford students, so best set Vivian on Archie and Archie on Vivian and leave them to it. Also, Shawn worked for Goldman Sachs, so into the playpen went he. (No further reason for hating Shawn, and none needed.)

'The whole gang,' Archie said.

Celine was glad to see Archie go upstairs. She stayed behind with this happy thought: Archie gone. Ambrosial. Sheer delight.

It was true that Luke hadn't replied to her text. It was also true that she'd just seen Luke's name pop up on Archie's phone. But life was beautiful, and she forgave Luke – and he hadn't done anything, but she forgave him.

9

Four glasses of chardonnay later and Celine was genuinely happy. She strolled around her uncle's house and dissected the symphony of sounds. Quiet upstairs – staccato. Each heel landed crisp. Where foot traffic was heavier, the notes slurred out nice and easy from a rumbling bass ensemble, and all the vibrations kind of melted together and it was smooth and creamy and deep.

Whatever you do, establish the midpoint. So Celine had learned when her four-year-old bum first met piano stool. Her teacher Ms Spillane hadn't phrased it like that, of course. Probably she'd said press the little key-key. As Celine advanced, the baby-talk morphed into proper English, and then a whole lot of Italian. Soft means softer than middle-soft, and very soft means softer than soft, and on it goes. But be careful. If the score says fortissimo and you bang with all your might, then you've nowhere left for triple forte – louder still. Celine had even encountered quadruple forte, which could only mean take meth and play it. She'd seen that notation, 'ffff', when she'd performed Hamelin's Liszt cadenza. That night she'd tricked her audience, made them think she'd done her most – until she hit full-forte, and showed her strength.

'It's herself.'

The voice belonged to Celine's mother. Celine started and turned around.

Brigid wore a cameo brooch, an ornate flourish on her otherwise austere gestalt. 'Everyone's asking after you,' she said. 'What a crowd. You must be thrilled.' Her tone was diagnostic. Brigid had an Irish mother's suspicion of happiness, and a doctor's reluctance to grant a bill of health.

'I'm surprised so many came,' Celine said.

'Ah, now,' her mother replied.

'What?'

'Don't be giving me that.'

They'd been having this exchange since Celine's childhood. Brigid always thought Celine was giving her this/that/these/those/them.

'I really don't know what you mean,' Celine said.

'Sure they're curious,' Brigid said. 'Intrigued. Nosy, in God's honest truth.'

'What about?'

'Mister Right. They've heard so much.'

From Brigid. They'd heard so much from Brigid. This was Celine's mother's problem, of her own creation. Nobody had asked her to go around trumpeting Luke.

'They'll meet him in time,' Celine said.

'Will they?' Brigid scrutinised her daughter. 'Where is he?'

'He'll turn up. Things are fine.'

★ ★ ★

Celine meandered away from her mother with those parting words in her head.

Things are fine. Things are fine. Things are fine, fine, fine.

If Brigid seemed tense, it was because her own marriage had failed. That wasn't Luke's fault. Celine loved having him in her life.

In that half-year's singledom between Luke and Maria, Celine's music had suffered. She didn't need daily chatter – she could save that for parties – but she'd hated having nobody to hold. She was a simple enough creature, and did better with kisses than without. Besides, Luke helped her with chores and bills. That wasn't a romantic proposition on its own, having someone handle her life admin. But when it was Luke – who listened, who cared – she wanted him forever. She didn't know the word for it in music notation: how she felt. The Italians, in their wisdom, conflated speed with joy, so that more joy was faster, and less was slow. But she'd leave that decision to the organist at the church – how much joy to give the march, or how long to draw it out.

★ ★ ★

'Safe home,' Celine told her cousin Sorcha's husband, and hugged him. He grabbed her tit and she pretended not to notice.

'Tell Luke I was asking after him,' Sorcha herself said. 'If you can track him down before the wedding.'

'I will,' Celine said, with the brightest smile.

Next Celine saw off Luke's friends. Vivian, lovely to catch up. Shawn, long may you continue with whatever the fuck you do. Archie – left without saying goodbye. Thank you. Someone gets it.

Why did Luke text Archie and not her?

But it was nothing. She'd leave it be.

★ ★ ★

In the blue reception room to the left of the entrance hall, various inspired persons had left wine glasses on Celine's uncle's piano. Luckily the lid was closed. She hadn't played tonight. The guests would have talked over her, and anyway, she didn't like performing for people she knew. At professional gigs, it seemed fair enough that the audience only cared to see the endpoint. But shouldn't friends want to observe her process? Shouldn't family?

'How do you do it?' they asked. Before she could respond, they told her: 'You're a natural.'

They meant well, but their fantasy of effortless brilliance interested them more than her actual daily slog.

Not even Luke really liked hearing what she did. The electric Yamaha in the flat came with headphones, and she wore them when Luke was home. Nobody on the planet could tolerate hours of scales in a thirty-five-square-metre box. He attended her concerts, and believed that in doing so he witnessed the most important part of her practice. To Celine herself, the performance was merely a full stop.

She couldn't blame him for wanting magic. Still, playing for loved ones made her lonely. No matter how well they knew her, they chose mystique; chose the movies; chose to see her through strangers' eyes.

Over the three years of their relationship, Celine had developed an elaborate, would-obviously-never-happen fantasy of just being done having sex with Luke when her phone rang. It would be a pianist – someone of Martha Argerich's standing – but not Martha Argerich – had to be a man – but no specific doyen excited her – so she kept him anonymous. She heard the ringtone on the bedside table, and told Luke: 'It's [Celebrated Musician] again, he's been trying to fuck me all year, will I put him on loudspeaker?'

– and without waiting for Luke's assent, she did so, and said: 'Hi, [Celebrated Musician], I've just had sex and you're on loudspeaker,' and proceeded to play them off each other.

It was everything she wanted. Someone who understood her, and someone she liked to touch. She'd never found all that in one person. But Luke showed promise on both fronts – and if they spent their lives together, then surely –

IO

Uncle Grellan helped Celine eject the last few guests from The Birches. 'Would it be a long drive home you've there now boyo?' – not the height of subtlety but he added filler.

After ushering Grandaunt Bernadette out the door – small woman, but no small task – Grellan turned to Celine in the entrance. His face had reddened over the past few hours, and his voice was husky from pleasing the crowd. Under his breath, he said: 'Is it coffee himself is off getting?'

'Who's himself?' Celine said, though she knew Grellan meant Luke.

Grellan regarded coffee as Luke's shtick, his leitmotif. He seemed to think nobody else drank it. When Celine had mentioned last year that Luke was bisexual, Grellan had replied: 'Ah, there you go' – then, seeing Celine's bewilderment: 'The coffee.' Celine was still unsure if Grellan had meant bisexuals were apt to enjoy coffee, bisexuals were merely likelier to disclose such a preference should they have it, or coffee made one in fact bisexual. It certainly made one anxious.

'I don't know where Luke went,' Celine told Grellan.

'Would he be off buying coffee beans?'

'No.'

'To put in the silver lad?'

'No.'

'And turn the little wheel?'

The 'silver lad' was Luke's coffee grinder, though Grellan seemed to have but an imperfect understanding of how the thing actually worked. Celine was fairly certain, for instance, that no wheel was involved.

Her uncle resumed kicking out the guests, and Celine looked around the front hall. Her sister Phoebe was no-where to be seen – she'd come out with some rubbish earlier about going to look for Luke, but she was probably smoking cigarettes in a ditch. Aunt Maggy, in her leopard-print dress, bickered with Celine's mother Brigid by the staircase. Grellan was the only McGaw to be relied on.

But he couldn't fix everything.

She needed to talk to Luke.

II

In Celine's first two months of dating Luke, he did the following:

1. Mentioned frequently and apropos of nothing that he didn't want a relationship, then kept coming back to continue not having one.

2. Took eight days to text 'can't do wed but free thu'.

3. Pointed out other people in the vicinity he found attractive, until Celine started doing it too, and then he found on reflection that there was actually no need to share such thoughts.

4. Had poor punctuality and then criticised hers. Did he teach piano? Did he visit pupils' homes across Dublin? Did he rely on western Europe's worst public transport because he couldn't afford a car in western Europe's most expensive city, and couldn't cycle lest western Europe's shittiest lanes break his livelihood-earning fingers? Besides, if they'd both arrived after the appointed time and he was there before her, then actually he was late first.

5. Accused Celine of having the wrong friends ('I mean do what you want, but Gráinne –?')

6. Accepted invitations to meet Celine's flatmates, sister Phoebe et cetera, and then always had a reason he couldn't come. It wasn't even important to Celine that he attend. She was simply offering, as is polite. Why didn't he just say: 'I am a twenty-five-year-old man and Western culture has convinced me that everything you do is an attempt to trap me and steal my seed'?

7. Had sex with Gráinne and didn't tell Celine. And fine, they weren't exclusive, but why did it have to be Gráinne? After openly disliking Gráinne for several weeks? Or was that just a front and had Luke already fucked Gráinne at that stage? Also, Gráinne wasn't even that good a pianist. And then when Celine asked, 'Why didn't you tell me?' Luke replied: 'I mean, the information doesn't seem to be doing a whole lot for you now.'

8. And, sorry, but the worst thing was that Celine was theoretically open to non-monogamous arrangements. She herself didn't have time for sex with multiple people – but she didn't care what Luke did. She just needed communication so she could navigate the potentially awkward social dynamics. It would stress her out just as much if he borrowed money from her friends and didn't tell her.

9. Celine vented about the Gráinne thing to Tanja, another conservatoire friend. Tanja replied: 'But why do you keep dating him?'

41

Tanja was a sensible person (when she wasn't saying 'You need to watch this right now' and then showing you a *Simpsons* clip from 1998) so this take on matters convinced Celine that something should change.

★ ★ ★

The conversation with Tanja happened on Saturday. The following morning, two months after Celine's first date with Luke, she took him to a large relaxed brunch place in the Liberties.

'If you want to date, we can date,' she said. 'If you don't, we stop. I want to date you but only if you want to date me. And if you don't want to date me, we can't keep messing around. I've just been through a bad break-up and I don't want stress. So we date each other properly or it's over.'

The waiter chose this moment to bring their Americanos. Once the man had left, Luke lifted his cup and drank.

'This is good coffee,' he said. 'And I do want to date you.'

So he did.

★ ★ ★

From there, things improved.

Yes, she'd pulled her hair out over him in the first couple of months. But didn't everyone, at that mad early stage?

What mattered was their potential. She'd seen it on their first date in that wine bar. Cherry cabernet, two greedy glasses poured. Their exchange about talent. He'd believed what most people refused to: she wasn't driven by praise. She made music, and the making was enough. Nobody else seemed to fathom that a woman might find the work itself more compelling than the social approval that followed. If he could believe that – if he had the imagination to see her

42

as she was – then that was enough. She wanted nothing, really; hardly anything; just to be known.

★ ★ ★

After nearly a year together, Luke had formed his own theory on Celine's approach to praise.

'So you know how I said it was good and you started breaking down what you'd done?' he said beside her on the creaky mattress. 'It made me realise you always do that. You find it boring to accept compliments, because you don't care about things you've already done. You want to do the next thing. So you deconstruct. How did I do that? Why did it work?'

The pattern he'd identified was that she never just said thank you to a postcoital compliment.

Instead she said things like: I think moaning helps me get off because then I breathe deeper and I contract all the way down.

Or: I got better at giving head once I started doing a kind of open pout with my lips instead of wrapping them back over teeth.

Or: What I've figured out with handjobs is you want dexterity but you need tension throughout the arm, like with piano.

It turned out this was weird.

Not everyone he'd been with had responded in this fashion when he said they were good. Apparently you could take it as: Hope you enjoyed, too, and now want sleep.

'Sorry, oh my God,' Celine said. 'I'll stop.'

Luke replied: 'Don't stop. It's you.'

And that, in their first year, was when she knew she loved him.

It wasn't conscious on her part, the dissection. She only

did it when she felt secure – and feeling secure was rare. With most people, she just said thank you. If they gave her a compliment, she responded with platitudes and that was that, because she didn't know if they'd enjoy a post-hoc analysis. But then she couldn't appreciate the praise because she was busy being someone else, all in case she bored the other person with her real self.

It had taken a while to get there with Luke, to the break-it-down-aloud stage.

For most of their first year together, she couldn't relax. She feared in the pit of her stomach that she was texting too much – asking to see him too much – saying too much – and being too much.

Ten months into the relationship and a couple of weeks before Luke aired his compliment theory, he'd come along to Celine's performance of Liszt's Hungarian Rhapsody No 2. It was the piece that had caused her the very most headaches, and also the tingliest spine. Her ballet flats padded on the floorboards backstage, but applause anonymised their half-beats once she stepped into the light. Her face shone in the piano's polished ebony.

Later, Luke found her at the reception. He wore a red jumper, dark like their first date wine. 'You were good,' he said.

'I modelled the cadenza on Hamelin's,' Celine replied. Then: 'Sorry, you didn't need that level of detail.'

It was a test.

She hadn't known at the time. But subconsciously, it was a test of whether he liked her real self. Of whether he needed detail.

He said: 'Didn't need, but do enjoy.'

And it had filled her up.

★ ★ ★

But maybe, somewhere along his lengthy chain of misde-
meanours, she should have dumped him.

Perhaps she'd ignored a message in neon lights: THIS
KIND OF GUY GOES MISSING FROM HIS OWN
ENGAGEMENT PARTY.

And his absence – what did that mean?

Unless she was upset over nothing.

Life offers few unambiguous red flags. More often, you
see specks of crimson dye. They could form a pattern. Or
they could just be dots.

12

'Sorry for not texting,' Luke said.

The party was over and he'd finally phoned.

Celine lay on the bed. The guest room was pitch black, so Luke's voice felt like something she could see. It was more than a sound to her, his speech; it was warm as well, in colour and in heat. It was safe.

'I got roped into a meeting first thing tomorrow,' Luke continued. 'They flew me back to Dublin. I tried to say goodbye but I couldn't find you. Anyway, just in the door. Madame Esmeralda's asleep. Well for some. Tell me about your night.'

'Lots of talking,' Celine said. 'Maybe too much. And I don't like shoes indoors.'

'The affected parties to shoes indoors are the home-owners, I'd have thought.'

'No, there's me. I have to watch.'

He laughed at that, which made her laugh too. She shuffled to get more comfortable on the bed, and put the phone on loudspeaker.

Did she believe his alibi?

Yes. She trusted his voice. It was odd, though, that Madame Esmeralda was asleep. Their cat was usually a nyctophilic little demon.

Before Celine could mull further, Luke spoke again.

'Tell me about the compliments,' he said. 'And what went on in your head.'

Damn him.

But she was lying down, and it was him, and it was the kind of thing they discussed when he was beside her.

'Actually I couldn't do a lot with the compliments,' Celine said. 'There wasn't much process to unpack. It was, well done Celine, you're marrying a man. And I don't know how I did that. You proposed.'

'And you said yes.'

'Pivotal moment, but little to say on technique. I had to come up with filler.'

'Had to?'

'Obliged.'

'Leave the filler to your uncle,' Luke said. 'He's good at it.'

'Render unto Caesar?'

'Almost.'

'But not quite,' Celine said. 'I've misused Shakespeare and you're dying to tell me which play.'

'How's the weather?'

'Which play, Luke?'

'It's not Shakespeare.'

'Leonard Cohen?'

'No.'

'*The Godfather?*' Celine said.

'Second syllable of *The Godfather*', Luke said. 'Kind of.'

First syllable 'The,' second syllable – oh.

Typical.

'I can't believe you're quoting the Bible,' she said.

'You quoted it. But yes. Do what your grubby author-ities demand, but don't do more, would be the synoptic take.'

Luke had studied Philosophy and Theology and had actually read the Bible, an achievement Celine found as remarkable as if he'd been able to speak Finnish. It was the first time all night that she'd learned something new.

But why on the phone?

Why wasn't he here?

'Luke,' Celine said.

His pause registered awareness that the mood had changed.

Celine continued: 'There's something I wanted to ask.'

'Sure.'

'I texted and you never replied,' Celine said. 'This would have been just after you'd left, and then later I saw texts on Archie's phone. Texts from you.'

'Oh,' Luke said.

Where was he going with this?

He added: 'I think probably what happened –'

Ah, one of those.

These were her favourite, where Luke talked about technology.

'– what must have happened,' Luke said, 'is I'd sent Archie those texts earlier but they only got delivered after I'd left. Your uncle's house is near the Tube station.'

'Yes.'

'I'd imagine – yeah, I remember. Archie said he was slammed at work but he'd be along. Then just before I left at eleven, I texted saying sorry if I missed him but

48

be punctual next time you law prick, we've all got jobs. Say it's 11.30 he arrived – Canary Wharf to Hampstead on a Friday night, easily forty minutes. So he's underground. And you know Archie. I'd say two per cent battery and he's on airplane mode. Then up from the Tube, onwards to the house, and only when he's reached you does he turn the signal on, and the texts come through.'

It had been more like 11.45 when Archie showed up, and Celine had heard him brag about expensing a client for his Uber. But inconsistencies were to be expected if Luke was unriddling an enigma that equally mystified him.

'Not that I was –' Celine said. 'It was just, you know.'

'No worries,' Luke said. 'But I wasn't texting anyone. Rushing to make the flight. Airport by twelve, boarded at half, and now – Jesus, 2 a.m.. You must be wrecked. Anyway, I'm back, and cat's asleep.'

'No worries,' Celine said. 'I don't mind it when you don't reply.'

It's a fool's errand claiming not to mind it when people don't do things. If you didn't mind, you wouldn't notice them not doing it.

Celine was far more willing to lie to Luke than she'd been with Maria, but surely this was a positive sign that she'd learned from her mistakes. Compromise, tact, et cetera. Besides, it was different with men. She couldn't say how, exactly; couldn't bear to specify why Luke deserved a degree of self-betrayal from her that Maria hadn't.

Luke said on the phone: 'I'll make it up to you when you're back. But listen, there's that meeting tomorrow.'

'Want pillow,' she said. 'But I should sleep.'

It was the argot they'd developed over the years, 'want pillow,' for when they were apart and she missed falling asleep with him. Want because want, and pillow because of the postures she assumed – sometimes on him, often around him, this way or that, intertwined.

'Want, too,' Luke said. 'Night. Love you.'

Between 'Night' and 'Love you', Celine heard something in the background. A slammed door.

Must be the cat.

★ ★ ★

After Luke hung up, she moisturised her hands.

At the guest room's chest of drawers, Celine smeared the emollient cream on her palms and laced her fingers back and forth. She'd never thought to imagine Luke when she completed this ritual at home. Why would she, when he was right there? But now she decided it was him, that he was touching her skin, that he was making it soft.

She blotted the excess lotion with a tissue, as if wiping tears. Hush, hush. Better now.

13

Two and a half years ago.

> **CELINE**
>
> How's Berlin?

LUKE

Cold

I bought gloves

Turns out they're 'Handschuhe' in German

Hand-shoes

So you're not crazy for protecting your hands
like feet

> **CELINE**
>
> I knew the Krauts had my back
>
> How's the conference

LUKE

See everyone thinks the most annoying
people in Berlin are the artists

To which I respond

Tech

          CELINE

          Haha

          Okay so

          I'm a very blunt person

LUKE

Yeah

I've noticed

          CELINE

          Except when I'm pretending not to need
things so men will like me

          Hah

          But basically I'm still thinking about that
thing you said a few weeks after we started
going out properly

          When you're like 'just to warn you I'm not
good at relationships'

          Because I'm still not sure what you meant

LUKE

You know what you said about harmony and melody?

Melody = main tune, harmony = background?

I think relationships have a melody and harmony

Melody is the best bits ... conversations, sex

Harmony is the boring stuff

Doing dishes, remembering birthdays, just basically keepign things going

*keeping

If you see someone twice a year, you can just do melody

More often than that ... you need harmony

And I'm shit at harmony

CELINE

Haha

I get that

But I feel like it doesn't matter as long as we're both shit at harmony

There's no imbalance then

So what if you forget my birthday? I also forget my birthday

LUKE

Never change

Unless I do, in which case change just enough
to catch up with me or you'll be the dickhead

Honestly though we're fine

I mean I know I've apologised loads for being
shit before we were serious

But once again

I'm sorry

I'm still amazed you forgave me

But I'm glad

I think we work

14

As the sun rose over The Birches, Uncle Grellan lifted Celine's suitcase into the car boot.

'With the gods on our side, we'll make it,' he said.

Celine hoped so, since they were leaving at 6 a.m. to catch a noon flight.

'Now you might be a wee bit early,' Grellan added as Celine fastened her seat belt. 'But get tea' – and he handed her a ten-pound note.

When she was a kid, the tea had cost a pound and the rest was for being his niece. Her mother Brigid had warned her before each visit not to accept cash. Then when Celine was twelve, she'd overheard Brigid complaining about another relative who didn't give Celine and Phoebe money when Brigid always gave some to that woman's sons.

'Mammy used to drill it into me to say no,' Celine told Grellan. 'When you –' she couldn't finish the sentence: gave us money. She knew now that the thing itself was fine, but you still couldn't call it what it was.

Grellan squinted at the satnav, despite knowing the route by heart. 'She was teaching you how to be Irish. A no, pursued by a yes. That's if you want to say yes. If you don't, it's a yes – pursued by a no.'

They were on the main road now, and Celine realised they might as well have been talking about Luke.

Why was she doing this?

Stupid question. She loved him.

Last night at the party she'd tried to explain the relationship to her sister Phoebe, who hadn't asked. During a quiet moment in the blue room, Celine had told Phoebe that Luke kept her sane. Without him reminding her that the physical world existed, she'd burrow too far into her own mind and never come back out. Phoebe had blinked, then asked if Celine saw Luke as a mindfulness app.

'I found out where Luke went,' Celine told Grellan. 'He's back in Dublin. Had to leave early. Work meeting.'

'On a Sunday?'

'Yes.'

'Busy man.'

They'd reached the motorway now. Grellan swore under his breath at the perceived incompetencies of fellow drivers.

'Sorry for the state of the house,' Celine said. 'I'd help clean, but the flight –'

'Don't be bothering your head,' Grellan said. 'When your aunt knows there'll be a mess, and sees an end to the mess, she's grand.'

He spoke like a man who'd learned not to chronically leave dirt in his wake. Luke, too, possessed this skill. Celine would never have moved in with him otherwise. Her own mess was okay, but anyone else's was intolerable.

'Listen,' Grellan said, 'is everything –?'

Celine ignored the question. 'Did you enjoy the party?'

'I did. Your man Luke –'

Your man in the Irish sense, that chap over there – not your man as in the man you own.

'You'd be pressed getting a word from him,' Grellan added.

'There were a lot of McGaws,' Celine said.

'Even accounting for McGaws.'

'Luke talks loads when it's just him and me.'

Grellan examined the satnav again. Driving seemed to distract him from his general need to fill silences. He was the opposite of Luke: he talked more the less he knew you.

'Your aunt said Luke showed great respect for her cake stand,' Grellan said eventually.

'How so?' Celine said.

'It looked about to topple, and the swoop of him. Swift reflex. Knows the stakes.'

'Luke's good like that.'

'As long as you're happy,' Grellan said. 'And as long as he pays his half.'

Celine and Phoebe were the closest thing Grellan and Maggy had to children. For Maggy, this gave her an all-encompassing need to control her nieces' lives. Grellan confined himself to statements of what the girls were owed.

'Make sure he doesn't leave before the vows, but,' Grellan added. 'Them priests do be frustrated as it is.'

15

1996: Celine Quinn born.

2007: Celine Quinn becomes Celine McGaw when parents divorce; at time of birth, father's surname was the obvious choice.

1996-2008: Celine McGaw exposed to the following:

- Books where women date or marry men (378)

- Books where women date or marry women (0)

- Films and TV shows where women date or marry men (561)

- Films and TV shows where women date or marry women (2 – *Friends, Sex and the City*; in both it's a subplot played for laughs)

2009: On a sleepover, Kelly Byrne, Éilis O'Connell and Celine McGaw discuss which boys in their class they'll marry. Kelly: 'Turlough Flaherty.' Éilis: 'James Skelly.' Celine: 'I don't want a husband. I want to live on my own and play piano.' Éilis's mother (having overheard): 'Ah now, you'll change your tune when you're older.'

2010: During lunch break at a mixed South Dublin school, a huddle of boys discuss how to make men come. In another huddle, the girls also discuss how to make men come.

2013: In one gender-segregated sex ed class at this mixed South Dublin school, the male teacher discusses how to make men come. In the other class, the female teacher also discusses how to make men come. But don't do too many men or they won't respect you, though they'll manage to come all the same.

2014: Celine McGaw's first sexual partner, a man, says: 'Tell me how to make you come.' She knows she's supposed to like being fingered, so she tells him to do that. He says, 'You like that, huh?' and Celine says: 'Actually, it hurts.' Later she realises she was meant to say: Yes, yes, yes, more, yes, oh [name], oh [name], yes, you're the best I've ever, oh my god, [name], I'm close, I'm close, [name], [name], OhhHHHHhhHhhhh.

2017: Celine McGaw and her girlfriend of nearly three years, Maria de Paor, attend a party and are asked:

- Are you sisters?

- Which of you is the man?

- Do you want a threesome with me [a man]?

- Do you want a foursome with me [a woman] and

my man [a man]? I want to 'experiment', a procedure one generally conducts with rodents. Also, it's vital my boyfriend participate – for science.

- Which of you is the man?

- So if neither of you has a . . . y'know . . . then how do you . . . y'know . . . ?

- Which of you is the man?

2019: Celine McGaw begins dating Luke Donnelly. On their third date, Luke 'warns' Celine that he doesn't want anything serious. Celine hadn't hitherto wanted anything serious either, but now she panics and scrambles to win him over.

2019: Later in the year, Grandaunt Bernadette tells Celine McGaw the following (in order of pride):

- You've lost weight – amazing.

- You've a boyfriend now – superb.

- You're a virtuoso pianist of growing renown – not bad.

2021: At Celine McGaw and Luke Donnelly's flat-warming, a friend teases Celine about her having 'stolen' Luke's freedom. This quip would be impossible to make with Celine and Luke's roles reversed. Or rather, it would be too easy. If you say, 'Celine is tying Luke down', you need to carefully indicate it's a joke. But if you say, 'Luke is tying Celine down', the words do all your humour for you; you can't possibly be serious. In heterosexual monogamy,

the woman forfeits at least as much freedom as the man –
but her agency isn't valued enough to be considered a loss.

Celine considers all this as her friend cracks their joke.
But she doesn't want to be a fun sponge, just spongeing all
the fun, so she laughs.

2022: The morning after her engagement party, in the car
with her uncle, Celine McGaw momentarily wonders why
she's marrying a man – but she doesn't much question it.

She's not an idiot. She's just been carefully taught.

16

It wasn't him.

Celine sipped her tea from a paper cup, and squinted at the man who wasn't Luke.

Black coat, black shoes – that could be anyone. Running his hand through his hair – lots of people did that. Queuing at an airport newsagent with bottled water and a sandwich – no, this scenario was too dreary to be his downfall. If he insisted on ruining both their lives, he owed her an anecdote at least.

The queue advanced. It was his turn to pay.

His head turned by enough degrees that she could no longer deny he was Luke.

Maybe he'd been planning to surprise her. Or his midnight flight had been cancelled, and the next one wasn't until the morning. But why had he told her on the phone that he was already back in Dublin?

There was no explanation. She'd have to trust.

Like she'd done when he'd seemed unusually affable with her conservatoire friends – not just Gráinne, but Tanja, too. Like when Celine and Luke had gone to Paris and spent the night apart, and in the morning she'd seen lipstick on his shirt collar. Like when he spoke to Archie and Vivian every week – in spite of having slept with them? Because?

But she'd trust.

She'd given him the benefit of many previous doubts, had spent the whole relationship doubt-benefitting, was an old hand and veteran and major-league doubt-benefactor, and basically knew the process and was fine.

And if she stopped trusting, she'd lose her march.

The church's organist would never hammer out Mendelssohn's chords. It would be goodbye to the flat at No. 23, and to the cat, and to all the life she knew.

She didn't want that.

So she'd trust.

PART II

The Bridesmaid

17

Phoebe wanted Luke in the Somme.

She meant that. She wanted World War I to happen again so they'd send Luke into the Somme.

It was true Luke was Luke due to the very same framework that had once turned men into cannon fodder. But since framework remained and Luke was still Luke, the Somme was the only thing missing.

★ ★ ★

Earlier that night, Phoebe hadn't been able to find Luke at the engagement party.

Shifty bollix. Tall, but. Should have been easy to spot him in a crowd, with the thick English head on him. He could fuck off with himself if he was pricking around upstairs while the rest of them got landed with Grandaunt Bernadette.

But there was Celine, sitting next to the piano in the corner of the blue room. Phoebe would ask her in Irish. That way, if Luke overheard, he'd feel left out. 'Cá bhfuil le garsún?' Phoebe yelled.

Celine looked up from the wingback armchair, wine glass in hand. 'Sorry?'

'Cá bhfuil le garsún?'

'Phoebe, that's French.'

'You what?'

'Garsún is a loanword, but "le" is just straight up French.'

'You're an awful swot, you are.' Phoebe sat on the arm of Celine's chair and took a swig from her sister's wine bottle. 'Where's your bitch-bastard fiancé?'

'Would you get a glass?' Celine said. 'I'm not drinking your drool.'

'Same genes. My drool is your drool.'

'And yelling it in English defeats the purpose of initially _'

'I'm finding him, so I am.' Phoebe gave a noble nod. 'I'm finding Luke.'

Why exactly, she couldn't say. To throttle him, maybe.

18

'You ask me, there are deadass eight faces,' Luke's friend Shawn said. He had sharp goblin teeth, eerily perfect skin and a habit of touching his upturned Ralph Lauren collar. Like the beams of a bridge, it sustained his entire self.

'Are there,' Phoebe said.

'Did I tell you I'm from New York?' Shawn said. 'If you want my opinion, I know, like, three girls in New York with your face. Or take Celine. You guys have, bear with me, the same face.'

'I'm Celine's sister,' Phoebe said.

'Bruh, I'm not placing women in competition. It's cool you've got the same face. There are only eight kinds so actually it's inevitable.'

'Celine and I are related.'

'That's what I'm saying. Same subtype.'

Nearby was Vivian – bright eyes, polka dot dress. Her tortoiseshell glasses perched at the bottom of her nose, as if she preferred seeing life at a remove. She turned around and said: 'Shawn, Phoebe's actually Celine's sister.'

'I thought you said white people can't say "sister",' Shawn said.

Vivian's voice was calm. 'So that's a few layers of you misquoting me. There's your normal one where I didn't say it and you're mixing me up with random people on Twitter. Then it's also on a topic I categorically would not have been discussing with you in the first place. Finally, there's this third level where you do it while ignoring the thing I just said.'

She spoke on the spot like Celine did, methodical but swift. Celine had mentioned to Phoebe that Vivian and Luke had dated as undergraduates. Clearly Vivian didn't know how to choose them either, but did know when to leave.

'Remind me why we let Shawn live with us?' joined another voice.

It was Archie, the lawyer who took a lot of drugs. Luke had dated Archie, too. Personally, Phoebe wouldn't marry someone if they had three friends and two were exes.

'I can't say why you let Shawn live with us,' Vivian said to Archie. 'For me it was: if you're jointly liable it's good to get a trust fund on the lease.'

'I'm right here,' Shawn said.

'Yes,' Vivian said. 'Do something about it.'

Shawn was too American to comprehend insults. Phoebe watched him isolate and twitch various facial muscles as if he hoped understanding would follow. 'That's really funny,' he said at last.

'It was very funny that she told you to fuck off,' Archie said. 'The way she said, Shawn, fuck off, and the thing she was saying was that you should fuck off.'

Now Phoebe could see where they all slotted in. They'd moved on from that houseshare, but they seemed to recreate the feeling in the air. As flatmates, they would have ripped the piss out of each other constantly. Vivian, Luke and Archie gave as good as they got, and Shawn absorbed plenty extra. Phoebe knew how they felt, because she had it with Celine: once you'd lived with someone, that space came to life whenever you saw them.

★ ★ ★

Phoebe had only ever wanted to have a good time.

When she was five, Brigid had bought her a baby cello so she could accompany Celine at recitals. Many screeches, one broken string and a livid tutor later – he left Moscow, and for this? – the instrument was sold and Phoebe was sent to ballet.

In the dance hall, she wouldn't move. 'No quiero bailar,' she said. The teacher was baffled until it emerged Phoebe had been watching *Dora the Explorer*.

From this, Brigid concluded that her younger daughter was in fact an aspiring polyglot. She sent Phoebe to Spanish lessons, which Phoebe hated because several of her classmates had an actual Spanish parent. Even at six, she knew injustice when she saw it. They got Spanish for free? On top of English? Muy bien or whatever but the whole thing was rigged.

There'd never been competition between the sisters, since Celine was four years older and Phoebe didn't care. A right pair, so they were. Swotty Celine and Phoebe the troll. Beauty and the Beast. Princess and the Frog. Only Grellan preferred Phoebe. She'd learned the word 'practical' when she overheard him using it to describe her. 'Great girls both,' he'd told Brigid. 'Celine would be for the books, but Phoebe –'

★ ★ ★

None of Luke's friends could confirm if he'd left the engagement party. Phoebe tried her mother next.

Brigid replied: 'Would you stand up straight?'

'I am,' Phoebe said.

'Straighter.'

'You've not seen Luke?'

'I'll tell you who I've seen,' Brigid said. 'Grandaunt Bernadette.'

'It's an easy mistake,' Phoebe said, 'Luke or Grandaunt Bernadette, Grandaunt Bernadette or Luke, but I was actually asking about Luke.'

'Won't you say hello? She's after flying from Donegal.'

'Direct from Donegal?'

'I don't know have they an airport,' Brigid said, with a face suggesting many entities could exist in Donegal and if they stayed away from her then all the better.

Uncle Grellan barged in. 'I heard something about Bernadette.'

'And what if you did?' Brigid said.

'Don't be forcing Bernadette on Phoebe.'

'She's my daughter,' Brigid said. 'Daughtreens are there to be forced on.'

The Roscommon was coming out in both siblings' voices. They'd grown up on a dairy farm that Uncle Flann, the eldest, was to inherit. Grellan had emigrated as soon as he could, and Brigid got a scholarship to study medicine in Dublin. Flann – 'Red Flann', since the town had several Flanns and he was the only ginger – had boozed away the milkery and now bothered Brigid and Grellan for money. None of this had ever been kept a secret from Phoebe, exactly. But the information carried an illusory aura of scandal that came from finally understanding what everyone had discussed throughout her childhood.

Phoebe scanned the entrance hall of The Birches as she climbed the spiral stairs. No Luke. Plenty of people she could ask for a cigarette – but Luke first.

★ ★ ★

In the upstairs hall, she paused at the window.

And saw him.

19

Three years ago, when Celine began dating Luke, Phoebe had just started university.

Brigid had wanted Phoebe to go to Trinity, but there were differences of opinion.

Brigid	Phoebe
Trinity is Ireland's best university	Trinity is Ireland's manufacturing centre of wank
Phoebe has academic potential best unlocked at Trinity	Phoebe has fucking legend potential best unlocked by being a fucking legend
Phoebe should study medicine	Phoebe would rather shit on her hands and clap
No need for that kind of language	Aunt Maggy says it

And Phoebe's Phoebe, and
Phoebe doesn't want to go
to Trinity

Phoebe wound up scraping into Film Studies at UCD.
Zero interest in the course itself, but the campus was
grand. She liked the concrete jungle, the brutalist slabs of
cement. There was lots of free beer. It tasted fine if you
had the good sense not to get accustomed to anything
better. She met other lesbians at club nights and crashed on
their couches; they all found her too fresh to want more.
Eventually she forfeited her maidenhead to a mulleted
Art Historian who afterwards warned her she was bad
news.

Days grew shorter, the campus lake froze, and soon
enough exam season loomed. This was unfortunate in
that Phoebe hadn't studied. Also, she had failed to attend a
single lecture and her coursemates thought she'd died. She
wasn't into tests. They weren't real.

Next month came a letter saying, blah blah blah, Phoebe
failed everything. She left it on the kitchen table, drove to
Cork with friends, and drank all weekend.

By Monday, the worst of Brigid's reaction had blown
over. Celine had dealt with it, probably.

But if not academe, Phoebe needed something else.

★ ★ ★

'Something else' turned out to be waiting tables in London.
Uncle Grellan had found Phoebe the job two years ago,
and she was still there now. Grellan's friend Jimmy Coughlan was upgrading his Irish pub to 'gastro-', and needed
'a girl' to serve the food. The ideal candidate would be

punctual, clean, and possessed of enough self-restraint not to be guzzling beer from the taps.

'Is there a story behind that last one?' Phoebe had asked.

'It might be that there is,' Grellan had said, 'but it might be that there's not. Jimmy Coughlan's rules come from sitting himself down on idle days. He does ask himself, "What would I, Jimmy Coughlan, be doing if I were employed here?" Then he makes a rule says don't be doing it.'

The restaurant was in Shoreditch near a cluster of tech firms. Jimmy Coughlan had stressed that the largely American clientele expected to be asked how their meal was.

'Why?' Phoebe had complained on her first smoking break with the barmaid. 'The customers aren't there to talk to me. Except the ones who are very much there to talk to me, but those lads belong in jail. Anyway, why can't they speak up if they want something? Why can't they use their human eyes and their human bleeding words to say, please come over, I need ketchup – this sentence any child can say. Or not even a sentence. More ketchup. A simple English phrase.'

'Ask while they're chewing,' the barmaid said. 'It pisses people off but they won't ask for shit.'

Phoebe had stayed with her uncle initially, then moved to a cramped flatshare after getting her first pay cheque. Her mother thought she was mad to hand over most of her income for a grotty room. But Phoebe needed to be free, even if she never saved a penny. To her there existed two times: 'now' and 'not now'. No one was right about the future anymore.

She had survived to age twenty-two with only the usual signs of wear: mild nutritional deficiencies, self-diagnosed anxious attachment style, self-diagnosed avoidant attachment style, stiff neck from excessive phone use. She googled things like 'wildfires europe' and 'heat wave crop failure famine' and 'when will dublin underwater' and 'will england fuck ireland over' and 'will WHAT IS HAPPENING IN england fuck ireland over' and 'why am i lonely' and 'why do i hate existing' and 'how many painkillers to die' and 'how much carpet cleaner to die' and 'why wont the government let me die'.

Google replied, DID YOU MEAN: WHY *WON'T*?

The search led Phoebe to an article titled something like: '17 household ingredients that might kill you, oops.' She'd read somewhere that the authors of listicles always chose a prime number to make their curation seem deliberate. She wondered if this particular journalist had added substances that were in fact harmless to make seventeen, or if they'd omitted a few because nobody actually needed the internet to tell them not to drink bleach.

Besides all that, her current problem was Luke.

★ ★ ★

He'd tried to be pals the first time Celine brought him home for Christmas.

The year before, when Phoebe was eighteen, she'd met Celine's girlfriend Maria. Neither McGaw sister had ever formally come out to the other. Celine had known for years that Phoebe was a lesbian because Phoebe had shifted the Bean an Tí's daughter at the Gaeltacht, an action so infamous that even Celine's classmates four years above all heard about it. But Phoebe only realised Celine was queer when her sister casually mentioned Maria. It hadn't been a shock. Phoebe tended not to assume anyone was straight unless they were really in-your-face about it, which in fairness a lot of them were.

No, Phoebe only felt she'd lost the run of things the following year, when she saw what her sister had moved on to.

Since their father's exit when Phoebe was eight, the McGaws had formed new yuletide traditions. Brigid hated cooking and board games, so they ordered Lebanese and completed a puzzle of Oprah Winfrey's face. The first year of this regime, Phoebe had complained. She'd been worried she'd have to go back to school and write about how weird her family was. But Celine had said: 'You'll get creativity marks without even trying,' and she was right. The essay earned Phoebe her first and only A.

On Luke's first McGaw Christmas, he kept asking Phoebe stupid questions. She tried to shut him up by speaking Irish with the others.

'Celine told me you work in Shoreditch,' Luke had said to Phoebe.

'In a gastropub,' Phoebe said, mouth full of baba ganoush. 'Cá bhfuil tú, Celine?'

'Táim anseo,' Celine said. 'An raibh sé i gceist agat a rá "Conas atá tú?"'

'You what?' Phoebe said. The tragic flaw in her brilliant plan: she herself barely spoke Irish.

Luke drizzled tahini on his falafel. 'Our London office is in Shoreditch. Maybe I've been to your pub.'

'The customers are pricks,' Phoebe said.

Brigid said: 'Anyone for vine leaves?'

'Pricks how?' Luke said.

'We started doing smoothies,' Phoebe said, 'and everyone thinks it's charismatic, I mean shows genuine personal charm, to want things that aren't on the menu. They crave unconditional acceptance and that's why they give such gobshite orders.'

'I can imagine,' Luke said.

He could not imagine. Who did he think he was?

'By the way,' Luke added, 'can I ask about the Oprah puzzle?'

Uncle Grellan had bestowed it many Christmases ago. None of them knew why, but suddenly Phoebe was certain that it was the perfect gift and that Luke showed his ignorance by even questioning it.

She'd never liked him.

Then, a few weeks after that first Christmas together, Phoebe saw Luke in a bar with that German girl Celine had studied piano with. Tanja? Yes, Tanja. The sight of Tanja and Luke wasn't indubitable evidence of wrongdoing. But by this point Phoebe had spent a year working in Jimmy Coughlan's gastropub, plying all its seedy denizens with booze. She could tell on sight when the ride was imminent. Whinnying to go, that pair.

She didn't tell Celine. Phoebe talked a big game – to herself, at least – about not letting anyone mess with her sister, but she was Hippocratic at heart: first do no harm. She couldn't see what good would come of ratting on Luke, meaning bad things would come, meaning don't fucking do it.

But he couldn't make her like him. Get to fuck.

With the imaginative head on Celine, that girl could love any bollix she wanted to. Just had to decide. Submit to the task. At first it had amused Phoebe to see Celine persuade herself that this cunty bastard was the one.

He became less hilarious the longer Celine kept dating him.

By the time they announced their engagement, Luke was nothing short of a tragedy. When he vanished at the party, a farce.

★ ★ ★

And when Phoebe peered out the window in the upstairs hall and saw Luke walking down the road with Maria –

Somme's that way, sorry but we're all out of helmets.

20

Phoebe's interests didn't always align with those of Archie, Luke's lawyer friend.

As Phoebe understood it:

Phoebe	Archie
Waitress	Lawyer
Earned £380 a week	Earned £380 a day
Did not suffer City Boys gladly	City Boy
Did not suffer fools gladly	Fool
Lived with six flatmates	Lived with Archie* *arguably worse
Liked cigarettes	Did not give her cigarettes
Not friends with Luke	Friends with Luke

They'd first met in Celine and Luke's apartment last year, when both Phoebe and Archie had been visiting from

London. The interaction had been mercifully brief.

But at the engagement party, one important thing had changed:

Phoebe	Archie
Knew Luke had left with Maria, but not where they'd gone	Did not know Luke had left with Maria, but could possibly track them down

Geography had not made them neighbours; history had not made them friends; economics had not made them partners; but needs must.

'Archie,' Phoebe said. She'd found him on a sofa in the front room of The Birches. He raised his eyebrows at her, then absent-mindedly patted his pocket. Was he reminding himself not to mix alcohol with whatever else he was about to take?

'There's something I wanted to ask,' Phoebe continued.

'Ask away,' Archie said. 'You might not get it, but by all means, ask.'

'I'm wondering where's Luke.'

Archie waggled a finger. 'Not to be pinned down, our Luke.'

'Archie.' Phoebe leaned in. 'You won't believe what I'm about to tell you.'

'I don't believe anything. Nor should you.'

She didn't have time for this. 'Archie,' she said yet again, and grabbed his wine glass.

'What's that for?'

'Listen, or I'll break the fucking head on you.'

Archie nodded. He seemed not to take the statement

personally, which somewhat softened Phoebe's stance against him. She'd meant no malice. She'd only stated cause (Archie not listening) and effect (fucking head on him getting broken).

Now Phoebe had Archie's attention, she said: 'I saw Luke leaving with Maria.'

'Who's Maria?'

Phoebe explained.

'Right-ho,' Archie said. He did a fair bit of that – talked 'ironically' plummy, which displayed a touching level of faith that the other party would understand he was not in fact a cunt.

'Can we find them?' Phoebe said.

She now knew her real motive. It wasn't just that she hated Luke. She wanted proof so clear of his many evils that she could do the impossible: tell Celine.

Archie said: 'If they're up to something, I'm not sure we can stop them. If Luke wants to cheat, he'll cheat. He's not a "paralysis by analysis" guy. He's an "internally condemns everything he does, but keeps doing it" guy, and those are way worse.'

'Text him,' Phoebe said.

'Text him what?'

'Text him –' She pondered. 'Text, "Where are you, you poxy bastard?"'

'He's not going to tell me.' But Archie sent it anyway. '"Poxy"? Are you Macbeth?'

'Close,' Phoebe said. 'I'm Dublin.'

'I doubt he'll reply.'

'If he doesn't, I'll trounce him.'

'Is that more or less violent than breaking the fucking head?'

'We'll see,' Phoebe said darkly.

But there was no need. Luke had responded:

Big hotel just off Hampstead High St

Hang on

(Luke shared location)

Honestly come save me

Am in worst conversation of my life

21

Phoebe and Archie walked to the hotel in the dark. The June air was muggy.

She asked Archie if Luke was generally evil to women. Archie surprised her by giving a fairly honest answer. 'Yes,' he said, 'but not on purpose. He's not a "hurt all women because he needs their love" guy. He's a "hurt only one woman because he needs her love only" guy –'

'– and those are way worse.'

Archie tipped his nose. 'Rather.'

It was another matter to conduct her own relationships with any such level of insight.

The lie is that women are good at feelings. The truth is that they're good spectators of other people's, and good coaches and good referees. They can advise from the side-lines. But if you drag them out to play, don't be expecting miracles.

22

Three years ago.

CELINE

So Phoebe

I just wanted to say something about Luke

Because I think maybe you've got a problem
with him

Like

You were really rude to him at dinner
yesterday. You must have known he was
nervous?? Spending Christmas with us for the
first time? And it's unusual for him to talk so
much in a group. He was trying

He said to me afterwards 'I didn't know you
guys spoke Irish at home' and I had to lie and
say you're really into Irish. So now he thinks
you speak a language you don't

Or rather, you speak JUST enough Irish to exclude people who grew up in England

When surely they've suffered enough

But it's not just Christmas

Everything Luke says, everything he does, you're always looking for the worst possible spin. And it's fair to be cynical about men, but you're actually being cynical about me if you think I'm too stupid to choose my own partners

Sorry, that was harsh

But could you PLEASE make an effort

And stop jumping to conclusions about him

23

'Phoebe, could I —?' Luke said.

She narrowed her eyes at him.

They stood outside the hotel restrooms, having left Archie and Maria at the bar. Phoebe had said she needed to pee, and Luke had followed her out.

★ ★ ★

Phoebe and Archie's ambush had yielded the desired result. They'd reached the hotel and found Luke and Maria in the lobby. The pair of them sat in front of the reception desk, both wearing smart-casual blazers. Maria's lipstick was smudged.

When Luke saw Phoebe and Archie, his hand jerked up to ruffle his hair.

The whole thing was shifty as hell.

But Phoebe wouldn't tell Celine.

She hadn't admitted it to herself until now, but the facts were clear.

Phoebe　　　　　　　**Celine**
Younger　　　　　　　Older

Train wreck (complete)	Train wreck (partial)
Who'd take her word over Luke's?	Even if secretly persuaded by Phoebe's version of events, would convince herself it was all grand

Celine believed things for exactly as long as she wanted to. Being smart, being logical, didn't help her. It just enabled her baroque self-deceit. Phoebe took the simpler route of putting no consideration into her life choices, but both sisters wound up equally mired in their own bullshit. Celine's decision-making required more cognitive energy, but not necessarily more thought.

If Luke wanted to cheat, he'd cheat — and if Celine wanted to marry Luke, she'd marry Luke. Talk about an impasse. Fuck's sake.

Besides, Phoebe still couldn't prove Luke had cheated, just that he and Maria had gone to a hotel. Phoebe could already hear Celine's response: 'How sweet of them to scope out a venue for the reception.'

With all this in mind, Phoebe had followed the others from the lobby to the bar.

★ ★ ★

Now Luke wanted to talk outside the jacks.

He charmed people by leaving gaps for them to fill. They enjoyed talking about themselves, and failed to notice Luke had left them with little alternative. This didn't work on Phoebe because she also let people talk. Eventually Luke had to speak first because he was both older and scared of her.

'Could I —' Luke said again. Here, most people would find the pause painful and say something. Phoebe did not, so he continued: 'I should explain.'

'Grand,' Phoebe said.

'About being here.'

'That's clear. We're here because you've got something to say. I want to piss, so let me know when you're done talking so I can go back to my thing.'

'I meant I've got something to tell you about me leaving the party. Celine doesn't know I'm here.'

'I know that,' Phoebe said.

'There's a lot of stuff I can't —'

'Then don't.'

'Honestly,' Luke said, 'there are things about my relationship with Celine that I won't get into, but it's best not to tell her I'm here.'

'Grand, I won't,' Phoebe said. 'Can I go?'

'There's context, but if you can trust that everything's okay between us and it makes sense in the overall scheme of things and if you can not tell Celine, I'd appreciate it.'

'There are lads at MI6 who talk straighter than you.'

'Phoebe,' Luke said, 'promise you won't tell Celine.'

'I promise.'

'Because it wouldn't be in anyone's interest if she found out.'

'I assume she will,' Phoebe said. A strange part of her was beginning to have fun. 'Not from me, but from someone. You're a marketer, which is to say a professional liar, so if your recreational lying is this terrible then I can only assume you want to get caught.'

'That, or I'm bad at my job.'

Phoebe's face went blank. 'Luke, you can't get me on

your team. You lied to my sister about this thing and probably lots of other things. I just don't feel like telling her, so
if you've said all you wanted to say I'd really like to piss.'

Now Luke's voice changed. 'Right from the start, Celine
thought you had something against me.'

'I'm family,' Phoebe said. 'I'm allowed have opinions. I'm
also, would you believe it, allowed to piss.'

In pursuit of this aim, Phoebe left.

24

When Phoebe emerged, Luke had already rejoined the group.

The hotel bar was dark, with huge armchairs and a strong smell of whisky. At a round table by the door, Maria leaned her elbows across the marble as if to claim possession. Archie and Luke held their drinks in their hands, perhaps fearing she'd knock them over.

'Celine didn't say you'd moved to London,' Phoebe told Maria.

'She didn't know,' Maria said. 'Not till tonight.'

The real question: why had Maria sneaked off with Luke?

Luke's 'why' was clear. He wanted to ride Maria because who didn't, and he took his chance at the engagement party because he had no soul. He and Maria had sat there talking in the hotel lobby because – here Phoebe was stumped. Would you not get a room?

As Phoebe turned the bloody thing over in her head, Maria complained to the group about her rising success. She touched up her lipstick with the aid of her phone camera and opined that it was all, well, a lot. Critics marvelled that 'her petite frame' could play Rachmaninoff. YouTube haters alleged that she had (personally) murdered Chopin; YouTube sycophants defended her so fawningly that she wished they'd go get laid.

'Not that I'm famous at all,' Maria added. 'But within my niche, an obscene number of people know exactly who I am.'

'It's interesting you chose piano,' Archie said. 'Did you think about trying the tiny violin?'

Maria said: 'I'm in therapy.'

'Over being famous?' Archie said.

'I'm not famous,' Maria said. 'But to the extent that I am, yes, that's why I'm in therapy.'

'Half of London is in therapy,' Archie said.

'The wrong half,' Luke said.

Phoebe couldn't tell if he'd meant the joke at Archie or Maria's expense.

'I'm not responsible for how people treat me,' Maria said. 'That's one of the first things my therapist mentioned.'

'Is she any good?' Archie said.

'So invalidate me all you want,' Maria continued. 'I can't choose how you behave towards me. I can only choose how I respond.'

'This valid, invalid stuff,' Archie said, 'it's drivel. Contracts are valid. Passports. Train tickets.' He warmed to his theme and slapped the table with each new item. 'Drivers' license, doctor's note, credit card, ID. Proof of address, Pythagoras' theorem, the law of supply and demand –'

Luke interjected: 'This sounds like the most depressing possible version of "We Didn't Start the Fire".'

'But all these things are valid,' Archie said. 'It's objective. People aren't.'

'Economics is objective?' Luke said.

'If you take the premises as true,' Archie said.

'Astrology is valid if you take the premises as true,' Luke said.

'Spoken like a Virgo,' Maria said.

Phoebe was only half-following the conversation. Celine's friends were all like that – full of screams and laughter and wild gesticulation when it came to theoretical disputes, but with zero ability to talk about anything right in front of them, about each other, about the space between their bodies, the breath they shared.

★ ★ ★

They were deep into the night now, but a jazz band still played. Archie and Maria got up to dance, leaving Phoebe alone again with Luke.

'Archie's got good balance,' Phoebe said, 'considering.'

It would be dawn in a couple of hours. She could act civil until then.

'He calls it his equilibrium,' Luke said. 'When alcohol wants to bring him down, but something else keeps him up.'

'I think most people call that being a cokehead,' Phoebe said.

'Every second person in London –'

'Not like Archie.'

'No,' Luke said, to Phoebe's surprise. 'You're right.'

The band played 'Well You Needn't' by Thelonious Monk. Indeed you need not.

'Serious question, Luke,' she said. 'Why are you doing this?'

'Doing what?'

94

'This,' Phoebe said.

'Why are you?'

'If I knew that, I wouldn't be doing it.' She shut her eyes. 'Luke, let's dance.'

25

By sunrise it was only Phoebe and Archie. Maria had gone home, and Luke had booked a room in the hotel. He seemed to have plied Celine with some bullshit or other about taking an emergency flight back to Dublin. No way could a man so useless pull that one off. But maybe he would.

Phoebe and Archie stayed up dancing, then strolled southwards to the top of the Regent's Canal at Little Venice. The boat shops were still shuttered, but several rise-and-grinders walked their dogs. Phoebe stopped to pet a Doberman. The middle-aged English owner remarked, with a mix of gratitude and disappointment, that he'd have thought she'd be afraid of his Rex. 'Ah, he's only a big old muppet,' Phoebe said. The man seemed not to catch her affectionate tone; with a subtle hand on her back, Archie moved her along. The walkway was tree-lined like Dublin's riverbanks, though the Thames looked marginally less prone to give you tetanus. (Small margin. Overall, both bodies of water belonged very much in the will-give-you-tetanus camp.)

Archie was grand to talk to. You'd hardly count on him

in your hour of need – but a decent fella all the same. There were people you could trust to be always thinking of you, and there were people best enjoyed in the moment.

'It's nice walking when everyone's asleep,' Phoebe told Archie.

'Quite.'

'But it does get scary when you're alone.'

It didn't really. Whatever happened, she'd deal with it. She tried, though, to express normal fears. Otherwise, people told her what to do.

'My legs are getting tired,' she said.

'We could go to mine,' Archie said. 'I've got a decent couch. Or we can do something else.'

'Like what?'

Archie gestured to the air.

'Are you always like this?' Phoebe said. 'Just –,' she waved her hands to show the 'this' that Archie was like.

'I'm not complicated,' Archie said. 'The key is not to oppose. I'm not opposed to finishing the cocaine. I'm not opposed to sleeping in my own bed and having a virtuous day tomorrow. I'm not terribly opposed to the sky falling, though I'd perhaps make adjustments if it did.'

'Is that your Luke impression?'

'Was it good?'

'Better than Luke's.'

The joke didn't quite make sense, but Archie laughed.

They walked further along the Regent's Canal. The water was still, and the pink clouds overhead made the stucco buildings look blue. Phoebe had been here before. She'd considered drowning in the river, and had asked Google if it would work.

'Do you ever want to die?' she asked Archie.

'No.'

'Not even a little?'

'I used to. I think what changed wasn't anything around me, but how I trained myself to notice things.'

'How do you mean?'

'When I was at Oxford, I tried to top myself, and I was comically bad at it. An utter clown. Then afterwards, whenever something felt nice, or even if it felt okay, I took the effort to pause. I thought: is this specific moment better than nothing? And it usually was. Once I started looking out for that sensation, I stopped wanting to die.'

'Got you,' Phoebe said. 'Your cure for being suicidal is: don't.'

'You're less likely to see something if you're not looking for it, is all I mean.'

Phoebe tried with the canal. Better than death? It must have been, or she'd have jumped into it by now. Why better than death? She enjoyed the river's patterns of movement. She liked two things really: things that repeated themselves, and things that went off balance and moved back towards equilibrium. The wet rings on the surface expanded evenly, but then came an interruption – a duck swam by or a leaf fell in – and there was chaos for a time, and back to order. Probably if she were Celine, she'd take all this to represent her life somehow, or to be making a broader point. But couldn't water just be water? Phoebe hoped it could.

Eventually she said: 'Do you think I could be happy?'

'You've got to try,' Archie said.

PART III

The Best Man

26

One Saturday in mid-December, six months after Luke and Celine's engagement party, Archie awoke with a pain and a complication. Pain: headache. Complication: stranger beside him.

The freckled man stirred.

Archie's East London warehouse conversion studio was his castle, and here was an invader.

'Morning,' Archie said. 'How's your head?'

'I'm dying,' the man said.

'I've got painkillers.'

'I don't want to steal.'

'Don't be silly. You're my guest.' Then the performative reach into the bedside drawer, followed by: 'Christ, I'm out.'

Sometimes that alone got rid of them, but the freckled man said nothing.

Archie continued: 'I'll go and buy you some.'

'It's not that bad,' the freckled man said.

'You just told me you were on the brink of death. It's really no trouble.'

'I can't send you off into the cold.'

'Don't be silly,' Archie said. 'Tell you the truth, my own head's a fright.'

He pulled on his things — cotton boxers, merino wool socks, linen shirt, jeans, coat with scarf draped around lapel so he didn't have to separately remember scarf — waved the freckled man goodbye, and slammed the door.

The winter wind stung his face. Did he have the man's number? Yes — he'd saved it last night under 'Freckles', to avoid admitting he'd missed the stranger's name. It would have been slicker, no doubt, to let Freckles enter his own contact details. But the smooth option was a stealthy beast, and only reared its head once you'd already taken the alternative stupid idiot approach.

Five minutes down the street, Archie texted the freckled man:

Sorry I'm an idiot

Just remember breed I've got tennis

remembered, even

have to run

I'll buy gear at the court haha i didn't bring any

Take your time though

The door locks itself

Hopefully see you soon

★ ★ ★

In their Oxford days, Luke had witnessed one too many of Archie's morning-after alibis. Eventually he'd snapped.

They were at breakfast in Magdalen's wood-panelled

Tudor dining hall, where they sat across from one another at the bottom of a long bench.

'You know it's not any kinder,' Luke said to Archie, 'leading people on when you could just say you're not interested.'

The boy did harangue.

Archie responded with a mouth full of cornflakes. 'I'll take you up on three points.' Swallowed the cornflakes. 'First, I never said it was kinder to them. It's kinder to me because it spares me an unpleasant conversation. Which brings me to my other point.'

'You said three.'

'I'll find a third. Second objection is that people say they hate being strung along, but they don't really. They hate rejection.' Archie took another mouthful of cereal. 'They wouldn't take any more kindly to an explicit "no". Actually, I'd wager the same rejection hurts less when it's implicit than when you're told, in as many English words, that someone doesn't want you.'

'Pass the orange juice,' Luke said.

This was in their second year, a few months after they'd broken up. That's what it was, a break-up, though Archie avoided using the term 'break-up' aloud. Nor had he called Luke his boyfriend in the first place.

★ ★ ★

At boarding school, aged seventeen, Archie had avidly consumed dating manuals that told straight women how to determine whether men were into them. Apparently, when a real man wanted something, he went out and bloody well got it – so your guy wasn't with you then tough luck, dollface: he didn't want to be. At this stage of his development, Archie had been nursing an obsession with the school's sharp-jawed Deputy Head Boy. Deputy wasn't with Archie and therefore did not want to be. But Archie wasn't with Deputy, either, and did want to be, so what now?

Then Archie had searched for non-fiction specifically addressing the 'man not sure if fellow man is into him' scenario. All he found was stuff about how to have sex, which seemed to Archie a simple matter of communication, spatial reasoning and rudimentary hygiene.

So Archie stopped wondering if guys were into him, and asked himself only if he was into them. For as long as he was, he stuck around.

★ ★ ★

This policy still suited Archie when he met Luke in their first week at university. But as they kept seeing one another, Archie became insecure. Over their first two term breaks, he went to San Francisco with three school friends, then to Delhi with his mum. On neither occasion did Luke give Archie so much as an I'll-miss-you.

Then Luke told Archie that he'd be in Ireland over the summer holidays.

They were in Archie's room. Their first year at Oxford was nearly over, and the days were warm and bright. The evening sun shone through the blinds and made golden rectangles on the desk.

'What are you in Ireland for?' Archie replied.

Luke stood opposite the bed. The corkboard behind him held Archie's over-ambitious to-do lists, polaroids of friends, and fashion cutouts from *Vogue*. 'Meeting family,' Luke said.

'Where in Ireland are they?'

'You're saying "Ireland" a lot.'

'I love Ireland. My dad's side's Irish.'

'You've mentioned,' Luke said. 'It's in Dublin my family are.'

'That's quite an Irish syntax.'

'The old country never leaves you.'

'Luke, you were born in Croydon.'

'Details.'

Archie fiddled with his bedding. The duvet cover was grey-dyed flax from H&M. His mother was a firm advocate of linen sheets, and Archie's budget had determined where to get them. 'Are you nervous meeting your dad?'

'I won't be seeing him,' Luke said. 'He's in London now.'

Archie knew not to probe further.

His childhood had taught him the main skill required for an upper-middle-class British man: how to tiptoe around others without seeming an outright runt. He was the youngest of four boys and had grown up in a draughty country home where his brothers knocked him about. His mum Anjali kept order as best she could. But she commuted to her cybersecurity firm in London, and whenever she was gone it was *Lord of the Flies*. Archie had learned to avoid clobberings through the rotating petty pugilism that constituted family banter. You started a million arguments. None of them went anywhere, and as long as you sided with one chap one minute and another the next, all was well. If alliances crystallised there'd be problems, but mainly Archie got through life at the house in Somerset by calling one brother a knob and the next a wanker, ensuring to vary it so each thought of Archie as his vassal.

It was different with Luke, whose brain seemed not to reward him for starting fights. Archie had liked this conflict-aversion right up until that evening when Luke said he'd be in Ireland all summer.

'Good of you to let me know,' Archie said.

'Yeah, just, that's the plan,' Luke said.

'When did you know you'd be in Ireland?'

'Last week. Maybe a bit before.'

You couldn't get anything out of him.

Archie stood up and walked the short length from the bed to the window, then back. 'I would have factored you in if I'd done that sort of thing.'

'What sort of thing?'

'Go to Ireland. But it's subjective.' Archie paced around faster now, and he was babbling, or perhaps he would have babbled anyway and his limbs were just keeping up. 'Matter of preference – do you consult people, don't you, sort of thing.'

Luke stood still by the corkboard, which combined with Archie's pacing gave the impression that it was Luke's room and not Archie's. 'What do you mean?'

Archie took a sharp inhale. 'Why didn't you ask me about going to Ireland?'

'What was there to ask?'

'I don't want you to fuck off for months at a time without checking if I mind.'

'Okay, yeah, sorry,' Luke said.

Confirmed: truly impossible to make Luke fight.

Archie said: 'Sorry and you'll change, or sorry and you won't?'

'Sorry, I won't,' Luke said. 'I mean, I probably won't. I'm not good with relationships.'

'But that's not a mysterious . . . you're talking about your own actions like it's a weather forecast. You're you. You're management. You decide if you'll be "good with relation-ships" or not.'

'Archie –'

'This is impossible. I'll still be your friend when I've stopped being pissed off at you, but I'm not having sex with you anymore.'

That worked for Luke. Everything worked for Luke. In bed Archie could do anything he wanted, strolling around Oxford's lanes Archie could lead the way, and when they looked at menus Archie could pick. In Luke's eyes, every-one else reached decisions easily and they were perpetually bothering Luke for his casting vote.

Archie decided that summer to remove his heart from the basket of items Luke would never make his mind up about. It had sounded like a pathetic excuse, 'not good at relationships' – but eventually Archie understood. It wasn't that Option A was unappealing, or Option B was unap-pealing. It was the very act of choosing that Luke couldn't stand, and if he ever accidentally made a choice, he'd promptly do something else to unchoose it.

* * *

When they reunited at Oxford to start their second year, Archie began his post-Luke pattern of seeing men for a little while and then dropping them. Luke seemed to find this hypocritical. But their core mentalities were different. Luke hated decisions and so never committed to an option but also never foreclosed on it, not if he could help it. Archie decided quickly, 'no' to this boy and 'no' to that boy and 'no' to the next boy. He just didn't tell them because surely they'd take the hint.

Throughout the rest of their university days, and for a few years afterwards, and come to think of it well into the moth-eaten vestiges of Archie's twenties, and actually probably across the remaining span of Archie's life, it was still a 'yes' to Luke if Luke would only say it back.

Or so Archie claimed. Another part of him suspected that he liked Luke specifically because Luke was unavailable. This allowed Archie to be equally commitment-phobic while pitying himself as the wounded beseecher. What would actually happen if Luke turned around and said: Archie, I need you? Maybe Archie would reply: Very kind of you, sir, but I'm dashed fond of my freedom, so I'll be off.

He'd never know, so he remained obsessed.

On and on it went after graduation, throughout their five subsequent years as London housemates. Sober, in broad daylight, Archie preserved what dignity he could. But with enough drink and surrounding buzz, Archie inevitably kissed Luke and asked if Luke was still, you know, not really down for a relationship. Luke didn't say 'yes' and didn't say 'no', and kept on being Luke.

★ ★ ★

Then Luke moved to Dublin three and a half years ago, and Archie began renting his East London loft studio with its exposed brick walls and cast-iron beams.

A few months after Luke's Irish relocation, Archie met Celine. He flew to Dublin at the weekend and joined Luke and his new girlfriend for coffee. Celine was short, plain-faced, dressed in taupe: the soul of inoffence. She wore black leather gloves, and when she touched Luke's face, she seemed to steer him.

The three exchanged hugs. Archie knew; Celine must have known, too. She didn't have any more of Luke's love. She was just better at forcing decisions.

Now six months remained until the wedding.

Archie had only lied to his freckled bedmate about the painkillers. He really did have tennis that Saturday, and would have to arrive early to buy gear. The court was in his law firm, a twenty-minute Tube ride away. A few hours afterwards, he'd be meeting Luke. The cocaine in his coat pocket would swing him through doubles, but he'd need to top up later or he'd collapse.

And then – before last night's 'yes' became entrenched – he'd have to tell Luke he couldn't be best man at the wedding.

A real 'no', not a Luke 'no'.

27

At the entrance to the court, Archie caught up with Kwame. He glimpsed the article Kwame was reading on his phone: 'How to Win Doubles with a Weak Partner'.

'Harsh, old bean,' Archie said.

Kwame put his phone down. 'We're playing Scotty and Salik.'

'Fuck.'

'Yeah.'

'We're fucked.'

'Sideways.'

Tony Scott and Hasan Salik were feared throughout the City. Middling lawyers, yes, but their tennis was murderously good.

The courts belonged to the firm, Pilley & Cluck, and were situated in the right wing of the office block. The men's tennis club met every Saturday. They had no formal league, no progression, no prize. You played to win the immediate match – unless you were up against Scotty and Salik, and then you played to salvage the shrieking remnants of your ego.

Archie and Kwame shuffled onto the court. They'd been

friends since joining the firm eight years ago, and Kwame – a tax specialist with spartan ways and a general sense of doom – had upgraded his Asics trainers only twice since then. Archie, meanwhile, forgot his things so constantly that he now owned about seven tennis kits. Eight, as of today. His new white polo shirt made his back itch: he reached inside and pulled the tag off.

Since the freckled man had driven Archie out of his own apartment without a gym bag, he'd stocked up at the Pilley & Cluck tuck shop. They called it that, 'tuck shop', though it was more of a sprawling supermarket. The store occupied half the seventh floor of the office and sold everything from condoms to – it transpired – tennis shoes. Whatever you needed, Pilley & Cluck could provide. Eighth floor: dentist, orthodontist, acupuncturist. Ninth floor: real doctor. (Archie's mother, sceptical of Western medicine, would scold him for saying that, but he happened to like taking pills.) Tenth floor: sleeping pods, where a non-trivial number of babies had been conceived. A partner had told Archie at his trainee interview eight years ago: 'You can live your whole life here.' Can – and must, given the hours.

Scotty and Salik took their positions.

They were an odd pair. Scotty was heavyset; Salik was built like a drainpipe. Scotty yelled and stomped; Salik mused. Scotty's serve brought you to death's door – and before you died, the last thing you saw was Salik's volley.

Archie was but a simple litigator. He defended oil companies against oil companies. Honest work for honest pay. He didn't have the cruelty for tennis.

The first serve was Kwame's, and Scotty responded in kind.

Archie knew how he'd describe the game to Luke. He'd

say something about poaching, something else about angles, and Luke would say: 'Honestly that sounds like a double entendre.' They'd often had that conversation at Oxford: how all sports talk sounded gay, to the doe-eyed ignorance of the heterosexual community. Archie's world of work became bearable when he narrated it in his head to Luke. Playing tennis to advance his law career – he'd typed out a whole iPhone note about that one, a catalogue of quips about the weirdness of corporate life. His pleasure in transcribing these thoughts came independently of whether he even shared them. In trying to make Luke laugh, he made himself laugh. It was as if his brain were anticipating a guest, one who didn't always show up – but Archie was still glad he'd tidied, because then he had a nicer room.

Kwame grimaced. The game was irretrievably lost.

But Archie would be seeing Luke this evening, and Luke wouldn't ask about the score. Instead, he'd want to hear about Salik's flared nostrils, a rare sign of annoyance – whereas Scotty's entire face constantly signalled annoyance, and the only question was whether he could signal anything else. Luke would find it hilarious that Salik wore his Rolex on the court. 'Is it vested with secret powers?' he'd say.

Archie didn't usually observe such details. He barely noticed faces. Although he put great care into his own clothes, he couldn't tell you a thing about what anyone else wore. His perceptions were sharper when he expected an audience.

And not just any audience – Luke.

28

Saturday afternoon, and one box ticked: tennis match roundly, squarely, pentagonally lost. Remaining task: tell Luke 'no' to best man.

First, Archie would pop back to his warehouse studio for drugs.

What to take?

Since age fifteen, Archie had never attended a party sober. He supposed there were non-alcoholic events that others termed and perhaps even experienced as parties, but it didn't count to Archie unless he was drunk. Not that he had a problem. He only drank as much as everyone else, besides the ones who didn't drink very much, and they didn't count.

When he went up to Oxford, both his partying and his need for on-demand mental clarity had increased. He added this and that to his spice rack: bath salts, molly, Cecil bien sûr, and the Ritalin stash of a boyfriend from Vancouver with three psychiatrists. At first Archie had believed the latter substance helped him focus, but he was only experiencing the initial euphoria you got from any new stimulant. Once the Ritalin stopped working, he'd asked the Canadian if he had Adderall. The Canadian replied: 'I'm not an ice cream truck.' Archie tried to respond that he personally would have said 'van,' but he couldn't quite move his lips.

Now, aged twenty-eight, Archie had no primary addictions and half a dozen secondary ones. So long as his cellar stocked a range of mood-altering staples, it was no great loss if a given vintage wasn't in season. His need wasn't to access a particular feeling, but to avoid one: sobriety.

★ ★ ★

The freckled man might still be in Archie's flat.

Hopefully not. It had been a few hours.

Archie opened the door. No sound of the man, and since it was a studio Archie swiftly ascertained no sight of him either.

Then Archie assessed his present needs as a parent would their newborn's cries, using external signals to guess at inner state. He was clumsy and not thinking properly, which perhaps made him tired. However, quick pulse and racing thoughts, so he'd best stay away from stimulants. If he'd had no plans then that would have left sleep as the answer, but he couldn't miss seeing Luke. He'd get stuck with being best man.

Maybe he still had those narcolepsy meds. Some idiot at work – was it Yves? French guy, M&A? Yves allotted Modafinil one-fifth of the credit for his scalpel-cut abs – the other four-fifths going to intermittent fasting, ketogenic meal plan, daily stomach vacuums and – Archie forgot the last one. Crucially, though, and the main thing: Yves had given him Modafinil that he now couldn't find.

The drug drawer was empty.

Freckled man must have taken it. Not just the

Frenchman's pills, but the lot. He'd even nabbed the backup bags that were stashed in an errant sock.

Could Archie face the rendezvous sober?

Like fuck he could. But he'd find a way. He'd do whatever it took to get out of the wedding.

29

'Tell me you won't have the stag here,' Luke said.

'Cross my heart,' Archie said. 'I'd say "and hope to die",
but I just played tennis so I hope to die regardless.'

'Scotty and Salik?'

'Crushed us.'

'Does Salik still wear the Rolex?'

'And a second one on his ankle.'

How was Archie supposed to date someone else? They'd
take ages to get what Luke already got.

They sat on a leather couch in the basement of Archie's
gentlemen's club. A Christmas tree stood under the central
chandelier. Luke found the place ridiculous, but he had
tired of lampooning Archie for being a member, so at least
the lectures had stopped.

The building stood a street away from the open lawns
and tall red terraces of Grosvenor Square. One hundred
years ago, the libertine founders had broken off from a staid
establishment after a brouhaha about the permissibility of
puce waistcoats. The police had tried to shut down the
new club on counts of indecency – but since the indecents
had already put down priceless Turkish rugs, the judge

sympathised and the carpets saw light again.

Archie knew very well, thank you, that private clubs were elitist. All the same, you needed somewhere to go. The moment anyone offered him a serviceable alternative, he would gladly take a scissors to his membership card. Until then, he refused to camp out in a workspace café like some biohacked freelance life coach.

'You're also welcome not to do a stag,' Luke continued. 'As long as everyone blames you, that's actually my preferred option.'

In the six months since the engagement party, Luke had acquired a new haircut and a faint layer of stubble. Granted, the five o'clock shadow probably hadn't taken him half a year. But the last time Archie had seen a freshly shaven Luke was during that strange encounter with Phoebe and Maria.

'Does Celine know you're here?' Archie said.

'Why wouldn't she?'

Since that peculiar night, Luke had been in London every few weeks for work. This wasn't unusual; his tech firm had always flown him around. Still, on each visit, Archie had asked Luke if Celine knew he was there. Luke hated the question but, as ever, was immovable towards overt strife. Archie probed deeper each time.

'You could do worse than join a club,' Archie said, 'if you're in London and you don't want Celine knowing. Kip out in the rooms, work downstairs – hold meetings, even. Total discretion. What happens in Mayfair, and so on and all the rest of it.'

'Celine knows I'm in London.'

'The next time you don't want her knowing –'

'There won't be a next time,' Luke said.

'Is that a promise you've made to her?'

'To myself.'

'Those are the ones you never keep,' Archie said.

Luke seemed unable to think of a non-confrontational response.

Only – for Christ's sake, Archie had mixed up the order of business. The idea had been to get drugs off someone and then wriggle out of the best man stuff. Fool that Archie was, he'd gone straight for the wriggling.

Then, in the far corner of the basement, Archie glimpsed his saviour. Yves the Frenchman.

'I'll be back,' Archie told Luke.

★ ★ ★

How many pills to take? Make it two – no, three for luck.

In the navy-tiled gents' cubicle with its own little sink, Archie smoothed down his hair and wiped his brow.

If he ever actually developed narcolepsy he'd be in trouble. He'd need enough Modafinil to rouse a mammoth. But the thing was, he wasn't rash on Modafinil. If he'd taken it last night, and not whatever he'd swallowed instead, then he wouldn't have veered into present straits.

He and Luke had gone for drinks yesterday after Luke had left his Shoreditch office. The thieving freckled man was there – a colleague of Luke's or some such bloody palaver – and a few other people Archie only knew through Luke, but Archie had still done most of the talking. 'You might know Luke,' he'd said to this person and that person and the next person, 'but you don't know Luke like I know Luke.'

Eventually Luke had joined in.

'I'd trust Archie with my life,' Luke had said. 'That's why I'm honoured, in fact speechless –'

'Well-spoken for a speechless man, but speechless,' Archie had said.

'Speechless with delight that Archit Patel Stopford, despite the hurdles, has agreed to be best man at my wedding.'

Archie had played along. Later in the cab he'd told Luke he'd actually do it.

Dire. Dire, dire, dire.

But he'd put things right. He had just ingested a substance that could kick a corpse into the quadrille. Give it two more minutes and he'd be ready.

★ ★ ★

Better begin as soon as he'd sat back down.

Above the cherub-carved mantelpiece was a clock that read 8 p.m..

Archie leaned on the arm of the couch. 'Luke, I've been thinking.'

'I'm sorry to hear that,' Luke said. 'Get well soon.'

'I've been thinking about the wedding. I'm thinking maybe I shouldn't be best man.'

Luke's tone was relaxed. 'What's on your mind?'

'Well,' Archie said, 'sceptics might point out that I'm the only person besides Celine you've had a significant –'

'I've had other relationships.'

'Significant, Luke. They've got to signify.'

'What makes you so sure there's been no one else?'

'If they signified, I'd have met them.'

'Vivian.'

'That was three dates.'

'I'm still not sure what your problem is,' Luke said. 'If you're going to be like this, why come to the wedding at all?'

'You're right. I shouldn't.'

The club's other members drank coffee, played chess, laughed. The Christmas spirit had visited them early. That, or their bonuses were in.

'Archie.' Luke looked straight ahead. 'I need you there.'

'Celine should be enough for you.'

'This isn't about Celine.'

'If she's not enough then don't marry her.'

Rather coldly, Luke said: 'Thanks for the advice.'

'I'm not trying to interfere,' Archie said.

'Then don't.'

'But I can't watch you marry Celine.'

'Why?'

'You know why,' Archie said, and left.

30

Archie had texted the Kaiser, and reached his apartment block just before nine. It was freezing as he left the cab.

The Kaiser was either Belgian or Polish. Nobody was sure, so they gave him a nickname that was only one border off either way. To Archie's knowledge, not a soul had dared tell the Kaiser why he was called the Kaiser. The man accepted his title with poise. He lived in Knightsbridge and was frightfully loud about the address; you'd want to be when the place itself was so grubby. But the location was convenient when, for instance, you were fleeing Mayfair and wanted to forget you existed.

The elevator creaked, and had a musty smell. The bell of No. 38 was broken, so Archie knocked, and the Kaiser opened the door. He was two metres tall, which made his poky residence a particularly comical choice. It was the equivalent of a normal person choosing to live in a hat.

Behind the Kaiser was a woebegone Christmas tree that looked as if it had been there since last year. So, in fairness, did its owner.

'I'm not in a Yuletide mood,' Archie said.

'We'll put you in one,' his host replied. It sounded like a threat.

'Who've you got?' Archie said.

'You know Yves.'

'I do know Yves. In fact, I saw Yves a few hours ago. All roads lead to the Kaiser.'

Yves saw the wisdom in this and nodded from the window, where he stood smoking.

The Kaiser continued: 'Then there's – they'll tell you.'

By the ghastly couch to the left of the room, one woman sat on another's lap. The undermost said: 'What time is it?'

Archie checked his phone. 'Nine o'clock.'

'This boy's good,' said the undermost. 'He's very good.'

'I only admit the best,' the Kaiser said.

'So it's the five of us?' Archie said.

'One more,' the Kaiser said.

The bathroom door opened. It was Phoebe.

★ ★ ★

'You're a hypocrite, you are,' Phoebe said, and stretched her legs over Archie's lap.

Archie hadn't seen her since the engagement party six months ago. 'How do you know the Kaiser?'

'He comes to Jimmy Coughlan's.'

'Yikes.'

'At least he's honest,' Phoebe said. 'He doesn't go around saying he's got life sorted, and then still end up in a kip like this.'

'That was then,' Archie said. 'This is now.'

They'd claimed the right half of the couch. The woman-woman compound to their left was quite undisturbed by them. Yves and the Kaiser had absconded, and the Kaiser had told Archie to 'man the ship' until they returned. Were people never done putting Archie in charge of things? A don's don, that was him — a capo dei capi. Humanity's CEO. Kingpin, key player and big kahuna of everyone's life but his own.

Phoebe said: 'You told me half a year ago you'd stopped wanting to top yourself. You said all it took was smelling the flowers.'

'I still believe that,' Archie said. 'Only sometimes there are no flowers, and you're still in love with someone you dated ten years ago, and the whole thing is miserable and then you want to die.'

Phoebe seemed not to know whom he was talking about. She inhaled her joint. 'You've no wisdom left?'

'You could try looking at sunsets,' Archie said. 'Sunsets are rather classic.'

'For feeling less suicidal?'

'Yes. Whenever I see one, I drop a few notches down the risk index. I've enough points to spare that I'm still up there with Marilyn Monroe, but —'

Phoebe toked her joint again. 'That's interesting, that you think that's funny. Anyone further back in time, I'd say it's fair game, but Marilyn's kind of recent.'

'You'll have noticed a slight pause before "Marilyn Monroe" where I was going to say —'

'Don't say it.'

'What's wrong with saying things?'

'I don't want to hear.'

'You must be curious,' Archie said.

'I'm not,' Phoebe said.

'Nearly a million people kill themselves each year. I don't know why you're precious about celebrities.'

'I don't want people talking about me like that.'

'You're not famous,' Archie said. 'You're also, as it happens, alive.'

'It does happen that I'm alive. It happens and happens and happens.'

'Would you like some Modafinil?'

'I'm on the straight and narrow.' Phoebe outlined her joint's dimensions with her finger.

'If you got that from the Kaiser, I'd say it has about as much marijuana as chicken nuggets have chicken.' Archie sipped his beer and added, thinking aloud: 'Stupid argument earlier.'

'Probably. Who with?'

Archie wasn't listening to Phoebe. Something had turned in him and he was talking and talking. 'I should tell him how I feel,' he said. 'It might ruin things between us, but at least I'll move on. Let me disclose something, Phoebe. Let me inveigh. This is important. The need to be chosen will fuck you over. Because if you need to be chosen, you'll keep going after people who'll never choose.' He put his beer down. 'Not the most expedient course of action, but that's what I do. I pick a person who hates deciding and I beg him: decide on me. Maybe it's that I hate choosing too. Maybe I don't want to be chosen after all, and if he ever did choose me, I'd leave.'

'Mind yourself,' Phoebe said, and closed her eyes.

Then Luke texted.

31

They'd come far, but they always wound up in small rooms.

First Archie and Luke had met in their owlish little studies at Oxford. They hadn't cared that their personal fiefdoms were tiny, because they slept in a tower and were a part of something grand.

After their degrees, they'd shared a South London Victorian terrace with Vivian and Shawn. Archie began training as a lawyer, Luke started his graduate scheme in tech, and they only saw one another on weekends. Shawn, the household's sole straight person, took satisfaction in working the longest hours. If he stayed in the office overnight, he practically threw himself a party, then called the cops once his own jubilations began to threaten the peace.

'I don't know why he's proud of being shit at his job,' said Vivian, who did not necessarily find it impressive when people took longer than others to do things.

Archie's London life comprised a few key elements:

- sugar daddies within legal profession who flattered themselves he wanted mentorship

- sad boys of Luke archetype who always texted back, which should have meant 'Luke without the bad bits' but actually meant 'Luke minus the intermittent reward structure that thrills the fickle brain'

- sad boys of Luke archetype who were as sporadically distant as Luke, making them useless to Archie because better the devil you know

- use of shower to steam tailored shirts; never ironed them; couldn't risk ruining

- Household Secret Santa gift (received): handheld steamer from Vivian

- Household Secret Santa gift (bestowed): snake plant for Shawn; 'Hey fuck you man I don't have time to water this shit I'm at Goldman' becomes instant household catchphrase

- number of times went AWOL from flat for several days, usually to stay at a sugar daddy's apartment, and told himself that nobody cared but it secretly meant a lot to him that they all kept calling and texting: 5

- times kissed Luke while drunk: 3

- times kissed Luke while sober: 1

It wasn't quite stable, but things had a rhythm.

Then Luke moved to Dublin for good.

He'd been floating the prospect ever since his first visit to Ireland when they were students. Archie had assumed this was to avoid feeling trapped – 'I, Luke, might seem to have settled in London, but the Dublin option remains live'. He'd never thought Luke would actually go through with it.

Still, Luke was allowed to leave. He'd found someone to take over his room, and handled the transition responsibly. Luke had never promised Archie he'd stay in London, and nothing in their relationship said that Luke had to factor Archie into his decisions. Indeed, nothing in their relationship said that they had a relationship. Which was bollocks when you thought about it. What else could you call it when two individuals related? I relate to you, you relate to me, but we don't relate? Claptrap. Even by saying the words, 'This isn't a relationship', you've just created one; you've jolly well instituted a state of affairs. Balderdash. Hate it. But it 'wasn't a relationship'.

He nonetheless managed to act chipper right up until Luke's going-away party. That night, Archie mixed gin with vodka and spoke his mind.

'I still don't see why Dublin,' he told Luke.

'What are you on?' Luke replied.

'Just a cocktail.'

'What was the spirit?'

'Gin,' Archie said.

'What was the mixer?'

'Vodka.'

'Vodka's also a spirit.'

'Matter of perception. I'll ask again: why Dublin?'

'Dublin because – I don't know.' Luke himself was fairly plastered. 'My mother's from there, so really I am, too.'

'You always say "mother",' Archie said. 'You can't say "mum" because "mum" is English, but you know you'd sound ridiculous saying anything else with your accent. Want to know what else you sound ridiculous saying? That you're from Dublin. You're from where I'm from. I've got just as much right as you to decide I'm Irish and fuck off to Ireland.'

'Then do,' Luke said. 'I'd bet Ireland can't wait.'

'You think I'm joking but I'm serious,' Archie said. 'You're Irish to them if you stay in England and you achieve things here. Then they'll be the first to credit your Irish grandparents or your Irish parents or the trace of Irish sediment in your piss. But go to Ireland and claim you're Irish – forget it.'

'I don't care,' Luke said. 'I want to be in Dublin and I don't need your input.'

There it was. Archie needed Luke, and Luke didn't need Archie.

The following morning they'd behaved as if the conversation had never happened. Luke packed in his room with the door open. Archie said hello from the hall, and they talked about how close Dublin really was when you thought about it. At noon the four housemates gathered in the kitchen. Archie's hug lasted as long as everyone else's, and they all said their goodbyes, and Luke was gone.

* * *

But they always came back to small rooms, and the space seemed enough for them.

College. Terraced house. Hotel.

* * *

It was midnight when Luke reached for Archie's shirt buttons.

A decade ago in Archie's Oxford room, Luke had left it to Archie to remove his own shirt. That was the moment when Archie first began dreading he'd lose him. On their previous encounters, Archie's shirt had momentarily turned Luke into a creature of action. He'd wanted the thing off. But it would have been around this time of year, on a jagged winter night, that Luke fumbled with his own shirt first.

Now they were back where they'd begun.

'It's tricky,' Archie said. 'Concealed buttons.'

Archie often gave a low laugh in bed – barely a purr, but it distracted people. Luke had once grown accustomed to this and eventually liked it. Still, that was a long time ago.

This hotel room was only slightly bigger than the single-bed nooks of their student days, but it had a charcoal table-top and dimmable lights.

'Would you say we've come up in the world?' Archie said.

'Hm,' Luke said, and stroked Archie's chest.

32

'I have to ask,' Archie said.

'Then ask,' Luke said.

'I have to ask if you always pack lube.'

'You want me to say that when I got your text I ran down to the vending machine.'

'Yes.'

'There you go.'

'Much obliged.'

Luke's hotel room was fitted out with the same shiny minimalism as Archie's studio. But there were none of Archie's personal touches: framed P. G. Wodehouse illustrations, a ceramic elephant oil burner he'd bought in Delhi, and paper lotuses left over from Diwali, which this year had fallen six weeks ago in late October. His Auntie Aashna held a huge annual celebration. Archie had always wanted to ask Luke along. But the timing was never right. In their first year at Oxford, they'd only just started dating and Archie didn't want to seem clingy. In their second year, they'd had a fight – and so on. As each Diwali approached, Archie thought: I'll ask him next time.

Dawn broke through the curtains.

Archie sat up in the bed. 'Are we going to talk about –?'

'We could,' Luke said. 'We don't have to.'

So no.

Last night, as he'd approached the hotel, Archie had planned his speech. He'd come shivering into the lobby, wiped the snow off his feet, and ran over the sentences in his head. This needs to end. Please understand. We can't even be friends, because it stops me from accepting that we'll never be anything more.

Loneliness wasn't having no one. Loneliness was the gap between what you hoped for and what you got.

Archie had climbed six flights of stairs up to Luke's room because it would have been torture standing still in the lift. The sentences kept coming. You don't love me, so let me find someone who does. Don't ask Celine to marry you, freak out, cheat, then get married anyway. Don't invite me to your engagement party; don't ask me to be your best man; I need a clean break. I shouldn't be the one ending this. If you care about me, let me go.

All well and good until Luke had opened the door. Intentions shipshape.

But the room was as small as their previous ones, laid out to jog memories. Their old circuits fired anew.

★ ★ ★

Now London awoke, and traffic moved. Soon Luke would catch his midday flight.

There was nothing to do on a day like this but make coffee. Archie pulled on Luke's terry cotton robe and hobbled past the bed to the machine.

Luke smiled faintly.

Archie said: 'What?'

'Nothing. You. I like looking at you.'

131

Of all the hellish things for Luke to say. Archie had a specific and developed and presently very painful fantasy of waking up every morning to make their coffee. Dreams had no business coming true.

'Say what you will,' Archie said, 'but I wear a good bathrobe.'

'You mean you're a good thief.'

Archie carried over the coffee tray and sat on the edge of the bed. 'I can't be your best man now. Can we agree on that?'

'Yeah,' Luke said. 'That one I might have to concede.'

PART IV

The Groom

UNTITLED 33

So that's why my best man is Shawn.
   Hah. Scratch that.
   New draft.

UNTITLED 34

I'll keep this speech short because |

UNTITLED 35

I'll keep this speech short. I've got twelve hours to write it.

It's late June, 11.18 p.m.. Technically, it's forty-two minutes until my wedding day.

I, Luke, am alone in a hotel room near the church. Celine is at her Aunt Maggy and Uncle Grellan's house. She's probably asleep in the guest room, white dress laid on the ottoman at her feet. We'd booked my room for us both to stay in, but Celine's aunt intervened. Apparently we can't see each other for a full day before the vows.

I'm not convinced Maggy realises Celine's had sex.

Anyway, I won't see Celine until 2 p.m. tomorrow.

If I show up at the church.

But maybe I won't.

Maybe I'll elope with Archie.

Hah.

New draft.

UNTITLED 36

Opening

I'll keep this speech short because [insert some bullshit].

Thank Eoin & Brigid (Bride's Parents)

Eoin, you don't give a fuck about Celine. If you're here today, I'll be shocked. But my dad's worse. At least you send birthday cards, are gainfully employed, and have never once insinuated you've spent time in the IRA.

Brigid – you're a lovely woman and I don't know what to say.

Thank Nora & Frank (Groom's Family)

Mum, Mam, honestly I say both. All the kids in London said 'Mum,' but you and my Irish relatives say 'Mam' –

Frank, you're not here because you're Frank.

Talk about Celine (Bride)

I'd like everyone to turn and look at the woman sitting next to me.

Or if there's a piano in the room, she might be over there. Sizing up the keys. Are there eighty-eight of them? Slippery or matte? Other shit, too. It's not my field.

But I'll tell you this much: if there's a viable instrument nearby then we're all dead to Celine, and she'll absolutely not be at the table while I'm giving this speech. She'll be sniffing out the piano like some saucy potential mate.

And maybe she'll need one.

Maybe I'll leave.

UNTITLED 37

It could work – leaving her.

Isn't that my arc? Nerdy schoolboy → same guy at elite university who wears turtlenecks and has his fanbase → same guy in major metropolitan city with prestigious job, also the turtlenecks are more attractive now, don't ask, can't explain → same guy pushing thirty, which for some reason makes him all the more desirable to a certain kind of woman with far higher worldly success than self-esteem.

Forties – whatever, don't waste your twenties thinking about those. But thirties as concept, thirties as experience, thirties as reality and vision and dream: as I near that luxurious decade, I approach my kingdom.

So I'll be fine. Can't say as much for the people I move on from her with, but karma chameleon, you come and go, unclear how emptying my hurt into random third parties and then blocking their numbers will help me heal but fuck off.

I've strategised my exit.

Just need to leave.

Just need to voluntarily leave my favourite human with the most beautiful consciousness I've ever known.

UNTITLED 38

A little past midnight now, and still no groom's speech.

Fourteen hours till the wedding.

Honestly I have no idea how Celine has put up with me for so long.

But here's my theory.

★ ★ ★

The first time Celine asked me up to her Dublin apartment, she made tea. The moon shone through the lace-curtained window. The kettle hummed. Her flatmates had assigned her the highest cabinet shelf, which she could only access by ladder.

'And Paddy's tall,' she said as she unfolded the steps. 'So why can't he just –'

I was workshopping a non-dickish way to say: I'm also tall, so why don't I just – but she was already on the ladder, reaching.

She handed me a Mozart mug. 'It's from my Uncle Grellan. He tries to take an interest.'

'The wig's kind of a let-down,' I said. 'I mean, compared to the Amadeus movie.'

Celine reached for a second mug, and I wrapped my

arms around her from behind. She was slightly taller than me now, thanks to the ladder, and she laughed as she turned her head. 'I don't know why it's funny,' she said. 'You being all the way down there.'

Her dress was soft white cotton. I traced the embroidered cutouts along her torso. She kissed the top of my head, giggled again at her unwonted vantage point. Her foot shuffled on the step but she kept her balance.

I knew all I needed to know then.

Celine and I both love details, but in different ways.

Her love of detail is sated through piano. She squints at scores, strokes keys. But re: her physical interactions with the broader world, abstraction saves time; is efficient; lets her get back to making music.

Ask Celine to describe me, she'll give you the vaguest adjectives. 'Handsome' or whatever. She can't tell you that I slouch, or that I bring a brown satchel to work. That I like my toast slightly burnt. That I find it irksome when book blurbs say right at the end: 'It's also very funny', as if humour were an afterthought and not the central force that prevents us from killing a) each other, and b) ourselves. That I can give you a full verbatim recital of the scene in Martin Scorsese's *Goodfellas* where a gangster describes his mother's oil painting. One dog goes one way, and the other dog goes the other way . . .

I'm a whole person, is what I'm saying. But to Celine, I'm a prop. That's all she needs.

Once Celine likes the idea of something, it can reek and pinch and clang and she'll barely notice. If you've sold her on a concept, you've sold the lot.

Whereas my career is the abstraction in my life. I don't, in flesh, want to be at my office – so I make a meal of techspeak, the jargon I fork away from con-text. I survive through language at this job I hate doing that consumes the greater part of my waking hours. In the rest of my existence, I look for tangibility. Wouldn't you?

I can hate the idea of my relationship with Celine. But if I like to feel her skin through her dress's embroidered slits while lemon tea brews in her Mozart mug – then I'll stay.

★ ★ ★

In those early days, I was the boss.

This truly wasn't apparent to me at the time. My assumption was I'd fuck it up, so I thought I'd say up front: I'll fuck it up. Except I didn't put it that way. I said: 'I don't want anything serious.'

Knowing Celine as I do now, I realise my phraseology must have kicked her into change-Luke's-mind mode. So did the rest of my behaviour. All the Archie stuff. The flakiness. And the thing is, two Archies can't date for very long because then nobody texts and the whole thing dries up. But if you've got one Archie, plus another person who thinks it's their job to make the Archie treat them better – then yeah.

She was more fascinated by my 'Read 4 days ago' than she ever could have been by a response. The void was her kink. Try explaining people.

'Ah,' I hear you say, 'but you just told me Celine doesn't pay attention to her own life. Now you're telling me she pays too much attention. What gives?'

She's not actually paying attention, though. She projects. Burrows into her own head, constructs elaborate theories based on the scantest of data. That's not curiosity. It's pure fiction. Or as pure as any fiction can be. She's not interested in me; she's interested in her own analytical pyrotechnics that my presence happens to prompt.

Contrast this with her approach to music. There, the score comes first. She loves piano more than she'll ever love me, because she focuses on the notes themselves. Her ego disappears.

Probably she'd say I made her anxious. I'd say she made herself anxious. Neither of us is neutral, so believe whoever you want.

Anyway, she was jittery in those first few weeks.

Then she laid down her ultimatum.

★ ★ ★

High-ceilinged brunch place in the Liberties. We ordered two Americanos. When the waiter left, Celine sat up straight.

'If you want to date we can date,' she told me. 'If you don't, we stop.'

At the time, she sounded stern.

Celine has perfect pitch, and is tone-deaf. Speaking plainly is in her nature – but for her that's a vulnerable place. 'Natural' = 'haven't filtered' = 'what if it's wrong'. She feels safer when she's padded her speech with 'um' and 'maybe' and 'I think'. Dropping that fluff is a sign of trust.

I didn't know that four years ago.

Couldn't look at her. Anywhere else – left, right, behind. Pictures on wall, silver frames. Mirrors. Mosaic skirting. Benches, mismatched chairs.

Then the waiter returned – 'Here you go, lads' – Americanos. Dark smell.

I drank mine.

'This is good coffee,' I said. 'And I do want to date you.'

I mean, what else could I say?

I'd only just moved to Dublin. I missed Archie. Honestly I shouldn't have been dating, and I definitely wasn't ready for a relationship.

But I was gone on her since that very first house party. It was up or out – and 'out' I couldn't take.

★ ★ ★

Eight months later –

'Didn't need,' I said, 'but do enjoy.'

I'd gone to her Liszt recital. National Concert Hall, Kevin Barry Room; grey-green walls, parquet floor. I sat near the back and looked up at the coffered ceiling: each plaster box framed a round flush light. The audience applauded as Celine stepped out – black dress, black shoes, hair neatly bunned. (She later informed me that this took far less effort than a messy bun.)

She sat and played –

– and this, I couldn't follow.

As in, I know she was good. Fast hands, focused face. Ripples, then gushes, then tsunamis of notes. But I know fuck-all about piano. I've picked up a few things from Celine over the past few years, but you know when you're a kid and you think the objectively best paintings are the ones that look real? That was me and music. My test wasn't: How conceptually sophisticated is this artist? It was: How fast can they play?

I still loved watching her. How softly she touched the keys, and then she'd strike. Full-body enterprise. Spine erect. Arms strong and limber – you're never really one without the other. I didn't learn that from music, I learned that from my paltry attempts to be an abs guy, but anyway.

Afterwards, at the reception, I told Celine what I could: 'You were good.'

She replied: 'I modelled [gibberish] on [gibberish],' then: 'Sorry, you didn't need that level of detail.'

That's when I said: 'Didn't need, but do enjoy.'

I don't get what Celine does. Probably never will. But piano makes her happy; and that, I like to see.

Some guy in a suit tapped Celine on the shoulder then, and introduced her to his wife. She knew one of them from [gibberish]. They talked about [gibberish]. At some point the woman asked: 'Who's this?' and Celine said, 'Luke' – no context, no 'boyfriend' – then went back to talking [gibberish].

★ ★ ★

So maybe you're beginning to see why it took me so long to understand that Celine saw me as the boss.

Three events made it clear.

> **1.** She agreed for Archie to be my best man, back before that whole thing imploded. There's no fucking way she wanted Archie in our wedding photos. She just didn't want to say no.

> **2.** She let me off the hook about bailing from the engagement party.

> **3.** I lied that night about already being back in Dublin. I rang her from a hotel, and just before I hung up, a nearby door slammed. She must have decided not to hear. That, and she probably saw me at the airport the following morning. I'm not certain of this – she didn't quite meet my eye – but her head jerked. Rapid. How you turn when you've just been caught staring.

She never said a word to me about that morning. A year later, she still hasn't.

What did I tell you?

Sell her on a concept, and she'll ignore the thing itself.

★ ★ ★

In a vacuum, Celine's behaviour would be insane. She's a gifted pianist and general savant. Why would she strain herself to hold on to some guy? Especially when she didn't make any such compromises for her ex-girlfriend, a fellow virtuoso?

Answer: heteronormativity is a near-ubiquitous form of mania.

You've heard the phrase He's Just Not That Into You. If asked 'Why don't men commit?', you'll say 'They will, just not to you'; if asked 'Why don't women commit?', you'll say 'Commit what, suicide?'

(Your bemusement on this point is fair.)

You know Mr Darcy came around, and that it's Lizzy Bennet's crowning achievement to marry a man who was once rude.

Jane Austen was Jane Austen, and wrote novels that have elicited centuries of tears and laughter. She had an intellect so huge that millions still long to know it. Countless hours of human life have been spent gratefully enjoying the output of her consciousness. If you measure love by how much time another person can spend in your mind while considering the benefit all theirs, then Jane Austen is possibly the most adored woman of all time. And she still couldn't imagine a happier ending than a man becoming less mean.

Unless he's only being nicer because he shrunk in value. That's no use to the heroine.

So that's why the plot has Darcy prove himself, so he can stay a prize, so he's not gone down and it's that the woman has gone up.

And given the novel has mostly been enjoyed by women – and that's not to say there aren't men who like Austen; guilty as charged; but just in the scheme of things – and considering the fully understood horrors of Darcy's depiction and Darcy's life, it's difficult to arrive at any conclusion other than that patriarchy degrades men far more than it ever could women. It hurts and degrades both, but women get more hurt and men get more degraded.

Not that it's a contest. Probably there's no prize and everyone should stop.

★ ★ ★

I mean I know it's maybe jarring that I complain about patriarchy when supposedly it benefits me. But you know *The Crown*? The Netflix series about the British royal family? Not a single person in that show is happy. And that's not (just) because they're inbred ghouls. It's because the system destroys everyone who sustains it. Even, or especially, those on top.

★ ★ ★

Anyway, that's where I'm at, vis-à-vis bride.

You'd think Celine would have seen my early diffidence as a warning. Whatever about the unanswered texts, me literally saying 'I don't want a relationship' is, perhaps, a red flag.

But Celine has never met sheet music she couldn't crack. She kind of thinks people are the same. And in fairness, I wasn't going anywhere. Didn't want a relationship, no, but absolutely did not want to lose her. String her along, perhaps. Fuck things up for her, maybe. Not wedded to

148

net-positive life impact; flexible on that point. But I was her recurring-happiness-destroyer, all hers, and the world's insanities made me worth having.

She got me to commit. The recurring-happiness-destroyer's word and bond: a pearl beyond all human wealth.

Will she get me to the altar?

Re: that, we'll need to look back further.

UNTITLED 39

House party, Dublin, four years ago.

Can't remember the music. She'd know.

Dark room, but on the counter an amber lamp. Sandal-wood incense in a holder, newly lit. The stick burns and burns, and wisps away. Sweet smoke, thick smell. I see her; she smiles with her lips closed. Then she touches her face and I notice she's wearing gloves. I ask why. Regret it even as I say it – what if she has severe eczema – what if she's asked this question every day of her life and she'd give anything for a moment's peace – but that's not it. She plays piano. It's her job.

I should have asked to see her hands.

★ ★ ★

Like every other prick, I thought 'piano hands' were a thing. You know. Lithe.

Celine has actual piano hands. Nails bitten, because if she's playing and hears a click, she solves the problem ASAP. Her fingers taper: they're stubby at the bottom and thin-tipped, which helps her strike with force but move nimbly between keys. They're not especially long, her fingers, but the webbing is high and her hands are big, so she can stretch. Sometimes she practices too hard and her joints swell and the veins pop.

The skin on her hands is callused, though she moisturises at night. Every night. You try believing someone who says 'I need you right now' in the taxi and then she always, without fail, stops and does the emollient cream.

And believe me, it's not for handjobs.

I mean she used to do them, but then maybe six months ago – definitely after we got engaged – she said 'I can't fully relax because what if –?' – and she wasn't saying therefore-let's-not, but yeah. I'm not really going to tell a concert pianist: No, please risk spraining your wrist, I did it for most of my teens and I turned out fine.

★ ★ ★

I mean it's not the main problem in our relationship.

I'm just illustrating my point.

★ ★ ★

I don't want her hands. I don't want her daily practice. I don't want her constant financial uncertainty, refusal to go anywhere for longer than two days if there's no piano, and willingness to drop all plans when some pissant orchestra rings her up saying 'Please can you learn some Tchaikovsky-ass bullshit in a week?'

And the thing about protecting her hands – I don't know. I get it. But who took out the bins before she had me?

Honestly, who breaks their fingers from emptying a bin?

If she were a man, she'd be a prick. The haughty professor. Some woman feels responsible for him or she's depriving the world of his beautiful mind. And he's like, iron my shirts so humankind can know my genius. Tidy my sock drawer so humankind can know my genius. Wait until I've left my study and then kindly clean up after me, but make sure I'm done for the night, because if I rush back to scribble a note and I see you at the desk gathering my plates and mugs then you'll extinguish my eureka. But if I return in the morning and the plates and mugs are still there, my spark may well also snuff out. Its flame eludes me.

I'm not saying it's exactly the same in my case. For one thing, I don't feel morally obliged to nurture a genius just because they're a genius. I don't do Lang Lang's laundry.

I also wouldn't do Liszt's.

Incidentally, it pisses me off when Celine compares herself to Liszt. Her thing is like, 'Liszt lived his best life and had loads of pupils and still played for hours a day, so why can't I?'

Answer: other people's labour.

That's how Celine can be a full-time pianist. Someone picks her food and someone else sells it, or stands there while she operates the self-service checkout without removing her gloves. I don't know how to estimate, but let's say for argument's sake ten specific people? – twenty? – live in conditions ranging from breadline to slavery so that Celine can play the piano.

Not 'so that'. As in nobody signed up. There's no form that says 'Please write your name if you would like to harvest wheat in service of Western art'.

But that's the economy in which music is made.

This can be true, and it can also be true that Celine's got fewer servants than Liszt.

She'll have one less within a few hours.

Maybe.

UNTITLED 40

Am I sure I love her?
   Unfortunately, yes.
   It's 1.22 a.m. now. Wedding's in less than twelve hours.
   It's still just possible I'll marry her.

UNTITLED 41

Talk about Celine (Bride)

Celine, thank you for everything.

Celine, I'd like to th

Celine,

★ ★ ★

Celine, I realised I loved you when we'd been together a year.

We were in bed.

'So, you know how I said it was good and you started breaking down what you'd done?' I said. 'It made me realise you always do that.'

Piano, sex – doesn't matter. Whatever you've just been praised for, your automatic response is to explain how you did it.

I told you that, and you said: 'Sorry, oh my God. I'll stop.'

'Don't stop,' I said. 'It's you.'

I knew I loved you then.

Or thought I knew.

But do I really love hearing you think? After all, I don't like hearing you practice. Isn't that the same thing really?

Thinking through a piece. I mean, if we had a bigger apartment – but five hours a day in a tiny room? Hardly ever a whole score from start to end? Sometimes the same few bars for an hour. The same few notes, even. Sight-reading. Drills. Piano uses more of your brain than just about anything else can. It's the hardest your mind works. So if I don't want to listen – then, yeah.

Anyway.

That day three years ago, I decided I loved you.

Two weeks beforehand, I was already fairly sure.

★ ★ ★

We stood at the tram stop.

It was a spring morning in Dublin and the cobblestones glistened with rain. The billboards opposite us were papered with peeling adverts for an Abbey play. A busker nearby played guitar – badly, but with rhythm, so you couldn't help tapping your foot. His case was open and on top of the purple lining lay three gold coins, shiny like the cobblestones, and then I was back thinking about those –

– and you looked at some guy's leather shoes and said: 'The cracks on shoes are kind of like the backs of hands.'

I knew then we had the talking thing.

Obviously you don't know what that means.

So I can talk. I can achieve functional speech with nearly anyone, except when I'm hungover and then it's none.

But I do it for them, not for me. I don't need a good morning person. I only ever say good morning if someone else has decided that we're doing this. Sleeves up, let's deem the morning good. But all mornings are good to good morning people, making it really a statement of pessimism. We give the day that greets us a participation trophy because we assume it can't do better.

I'll never be a huge sayer of good morning, although if people are doing it, I'll get involved.

Celine, I regret to inform you that your maybe-very-soon-to-be husband has constant anxiety about running out of things to say. So if I'm with someone where the dynamic revolves around sharing information about people we both know – we might run out. Which you'd think one could accept. Just hold as a possibility among many on life's zipping rollercoaster. But obviously I'm like, 'What if this makes me a failure.' And 'what if' is being kind, show the old Luke a bit of love there, since I am never in any real doubt that I'm a failure. Hah.

Anyway.

At that tram stop, at any tram stop, we'll always find things to talk about.

You'll say something about a man's leather shoes – 'The cracks on shoes are kind of like the backs of hands' – and that there's symmetry, you know, hands and feet. Or if not that, you'll notice something else. And I'll think of stuff as well. I'll say, 'There's also a symmetry between the round shiny coins and round shiny cobblestones.' Or I won't say that, because I'm not a complete bellend, but anyway. Main thing is – I can make completely pointless remarks to you, and you can make them to me.

Because it's not pointless. You saying it is the point.

I said I wasn't a good morning person. But I think I wasn't until I met you. The day is never going to get me to say: well done, day, for being a day. But I do think you've done well for being you. And you're only here if there's a day. So I'll give the day its credit.

UNTITLED 42

2.14 a.m. Wedding's in eleven hours, forty-six minutes.

Got too tired to sit at the desk, so I'm slumped on the bed now. The duvet remains tucked. If I get under it, I'll fall asleep, and I'll wake up with no groom's speech and then I'll definitely bail.

Which would help in a way. It'd make the decision easier. Problem is, I love her.

★ ★ ★

How can I love her and be such a prick?

We need to go even further back.

UNTITLED 43

Talk about Archie (|

UNTITLED 44

Talk about Archie (No longer best m|

UNTITLED 45

Talk about Archie (Friend |

UNTITLED 46

Talk about Archie (|

UNTITLED 47

2.38 a.m., roughly eleven hours till wedding.

This is the world's worst groom's speech.

★ ★ ★

If he's here tonight, please turn your gaze to the man with the pocket square. The waggish scallop fold is a risk at a wedding, but calculated: the cloth's white and his tie is plain. Every outfit needs a hero, and Archie's protagonist isn't the article itself but its assembly.

★ ★ ★

In our second year at Oxford, Magdalen College sent ten of us to a Tuscan villa. Fucked if I remember why. Probably an alumni bequest. Some geologist died sixty years ago, The Honourable Geoffrey de Wank or whatever, and this was his dying wish, to pack off a few twenty-year-olds to Italy and trust good things would ensue.

We wound up taking Archie's Canadian then-boy-friend's Ritalin. Seven of us were buzzing and three were like, 'I should answer emails.' I was in the email camp, as was Vivian. We discussed with the Canadian whether this meant we had ADHD. He said we should consult a pro-fessional, since one can't diagnose people willy-nilly, and

162

then he offered us more Ritalin. Anyway, the point of the story –

That week, Archie explained sprezzatura.

He and I were alone in my room. His Canadian was off tasting wine.

'I can look at my clothes and make a plan of action,' Archie said, 'and that's panache, but you've got something better.'

'What?' I said.

'Sprezzatura.'

'What?' I said again.

'Look at your sleeves.' He held out my arm. 'Cuffs rolled up, but the edges don't quite meet.'

'I mean, it's not how I spend my time. Aligning sleeves.'

'That's my point. Quelle nonchalance. Oh, I just threw this on.'

'But I did just throw it on.'

'And I,' – Archie demonstrated his near-identical rolled sleeves – 'also just threw this on.'

'But you said –'

'I'm aware of every step. You, on the other hand, don't consciously register what you've done. But that's all in our heads. The external appearance is that we both jolly well threw the shirt on. You can't prove otherwise.'

'Archie,' I said, 'you started off saying you don't have sprezzatura.'

'Correct,' he said. 'In the course of my explanation, I realised that I do.'

And he does.

★ ★ ★

He's not a groomsman anymore, but he's still invited.

I wonder what he'll wear.

If he comes.

★ ★ ★

But I'm getting ahead of myself. Let's start with the year I met him.

★ ★ ★

It was my first day at Oxford. I'd got the bus up from London, and spent the journey taking notes on the social advice in freshers' magazines:

- leave door open when unpacking + say hello when people pass

- just talk, we're all in the same boat

- DON'T ask where they're from or what they're reading

- [own annotation: if you do insist on asking, then ask what they're 'reading,' not what they're studying]

My father allegedly came from money, but for details I'd need to have met the man in person. My mother worked temp jobs, preferred the more menial ones, said no career required her whole brain and it's far less tedious using none. Both parents were from Dublin, but I was born in London when my mother's plan to go off to England and get an abortion had been executed partly but not fully.

When I met Archie at university, I was just trying to get through my first day.

★ ★ ★

The Magdalen Junior Common Room was having a freshers' quiz, and I'm better at talking to people within structured formats. I don't doubt my ability to think, just

164

my ability to emote, so if the sole purpose of the exchange is to have an exchange – then yeah.

Anyway.

I waited at the common room threshold and only entered once things were about to start.

The girl at the sign-up desk handed me a label and a marker and said: 'Write your name and course.' I wrote: Luke Donnelly, Philosophy & Theology – lots of eeee sounds – and scanned for a team to join.

'Now here's a candidate,' someone said.

Deep brown eyes, sharp cheekbones, black hair. Then I couldn't keep looking directly into the sun, and instead peered at the mustard jumper and a tag: Archit Patel Stopford, Law.

'If you're Scottish I'll kill you,' the boy said.

Something funny to say back – nothing came. Finally I said: 'I'm not Scottish.'

'Therefore Donnelly's Irish,' the boy said. 'Yes?'

'Second gen,' I said. 'Both parents from Dublin.' I'd explained that one enough times that it came readily.

'Spiffing,' the boy said. 'Luke, I'm Archie. You don't have a team, do you? Ditch them if so. They may say I'm a dreamer. But it turns out, Monsieur Donnelly, I'm not the only one, having finally found person the fourth of Irish heritage.'

I wasn't yet used to Archie's facetious archaisms, and wondered who actually said 'spiffing'.

Archie led me to a table with the team name scrawled on a placard: IREL-AMPERSAND. Two others were already seated, and Archie gestured as he introduced them. 'Shawn, of New York extraction, several ancestors having fled the Great Irish Famine from County May-OH. Vivian,

Lagos-born, moved to Ireland as a child, then to London aged fifteen, gracing us finally with her presence.' He then pointed at himself: 'Archit to Hindiphones, Archie to Anglos, Archibald to racist cab drivers: one Irish grandparent, one English, two Indian, equals third-gen something-or-other.' Turning finally to me: 'Angels, our fourth. He's definitely more Irish than me or Shawn. Vivian's the most Irish, having actually lived there, but you could arm-wrestle if keen to resolve.'

'We're not keen,' Vivian said. 'Nobody but you gives a diasporic fuck. Luke, sit down before this eejit scares you off.'

★ ★ ★

I soon learned that in order to date Archie, you need to forget about him while he's high on coke or braving an essay crisis, or both at once, or God knows what. You've got to accept that for hours, days or sometimes weeks on end, he might be happy/forlorn/dead, and you'll have no idea which until he resurfaces. At this juncture you need to pretend everything's normal. His thing is: 'I find life so stressful that I can't be expected to communicate with people who love me.'

We went out in our first year. Then, just before the summer, he confronted me about making plans to visit Dublin without his permission.

'Why didn't you ask me about going to Ireland?' he said.

For context, Archie had at this point gone to locations ranging from San Francisco to Delhi without seeking my approval. Nor did I expect him to, but his entitlement – yeah, that was news to me.

'What was there to ask?' I said.

'I don't want you to fuck off for months at a time without asking if I mind.'

I didn't say: Then how about you stop doing it? I'd seen how that went with my mother's boyfriends. They skulked off, then came back and demanded to know where she'd been. One of them kicked our door in. The lock still jams. So I did what Nora does: take the blame.

'I'm not good with relationships,' I improvised.

You might say that coming from an eighteen-year-old, this sounded like something I'd heard on a soap opera. And you'd be right. Forget which one. *Eastenders*, maybe.

Anyway, Archie ended it then.

A moronic part of me had been hoping he'd beg and plead and say, no, Luke, I need you. But that's not what people actually do when they want a relationship and you don't. In real life, if they like themselves, they say, 'Well, bye, then.' And if they hate themselves, they think, 'I'd better go along with this'; and they say, 'That's cool, let's just see how it goes.'

So of the two options, I do think Archie took the better one. Draw your own conclusions about Celine.

In our Oxford days, I'm sure I caused Archie as much pain as he caused me. He recalls those moments in detail, but not the times he forgot I existed. That's the nature of memory. It's certainly the nature of Archie.

Here's how to be with him: treat him as he treats you.

The trouble is, I never mastered his modus oper-Archie well enough for things to work out between us. But I learned it plenty well enough to fuck up all my subsequent relationships.

Leaving Celine at the altar, for instance – that would be an Archie thing to do.

Next came Vivian. We dated for a few weeks in our final year at Oxford.

The first date – Christ. I took her to a terrible art film. I spent ninety minutes thinking, fuck, what if she hates this and blames me, or what if she likes it and I claim to agree and then we'll build everything on this bedrock of deceit. The last scene ended with a shot of a car driving along a harbour. I reached for Vivian's hand, and we sat there till the credits rolled. Outside the cinema, she said it was the worst movie she'd ever seen. It was cold. Her breath made a cloud.

My subsequent behaviour confused me at the time. Looking back, I think a switch flipped and I thought: 'I really like Vivian; time to do the being-like-Archie stuff, which is how all relationships work because it's how my first one did.' So I did that – the going AWOL, the bizarre inability to send a simple text.

No sensible person puts up with that. Vivian ended it.

'I've already tried to change two guys who are like you in every meaningful way,' she said. 'The puzzle no longer intrigues. I'm more into Rubik's Cubes these days. I like talking to you, but I'll get that by being friends.'

She dumped me so conclusively that I got over her fairly soon. It's easy to move on when there's closure. I'll never be with nineties Winona Ryder, either, or present-day Winona for that matter, who still has it and I still would, but it's not happening – and nor is Vivian.

As my mother says: sure look.

★ ★ ★

After our finals, Vivian and I moved down to London with Shawn and Archie. The first year in our shared house was the happiest of my life. I helped Vivian practice for interviews until she got her first art gallery job. At exhibition openings, she developed a secret eyebrow raise for when she wanted me to save her from creeps. We play-acted a different relationship each night. These ersatz partnerships were far more fun than the real one we'd attempted. It's what Celine later articulated to me as the harmony/melody thing, melody being the highlights. Vivian and I did nothing but melody on those nights – me in a dressed-down work suit, her in a cocktail dress. We nibbled olives and nodded at portraits. The harmony, the everyday stuff, would still suck if we tried, so we didn't.

Then Archie's substance abuse got worse and his demands on me grew. He spent his rent money on cocaine and asked me to spot him. Went missing. Came back, and snapped when I asked where he'd been. The worst bits of his Oxford behaviour all over again.

It was too much for me. That, and I was restless. My tech firm offered a move to Dublin, and I went.

★ ★ ★

Then came Celine.

Dated. Moved into No. 23 after two years. Adopted Madame Esmeralda after two-point-five, and got engaged within three.

Now, today, after four years together, we're getting married.

UNTITLED 48

4.33 a.m.. Headache; need more coffee, or maybe less. Too late for less, so let's try more.

About the affairs.

★ ★ ★

I slept with Gráinne, Celine's conservatoire chum, before Celine and I went exclusive. I didn't like Gráinne and she seemed like a bad friend to Celine – and, I mean, was I wrong? – but I could sense the talk approaching with Celine. You know. Do we make this serious or do we stop. I knew that was coming, because you can't indefinitely fuck someone on a casual basis. Nothing to do with morality. Just hormones. Your thermostat adjusts to them one way or another. You start feeling better around them and you get attached, or you start feeling worse and it's over. Both of these possibilities scared me, so I fucked Gráinne. Don't ask why I thought that would help.

Anyway, the Gráinne thing wound up forcing the let's-date-properly talk. And I told Celine: yes, yes yes yes, yes. Don't want a relationship, but can't stand to lose you – so yes.

Didn't say all those words but yeah.

Two weeks later, I fucked Gráinne again. And what's-her-face the following month – another conservatoire friend – Tanja? Who said afterwards, 'Fingers crossed she dumps you soon.' Deeply unclear if that's a compliment.

★ ★ ★

Three and a half years ago, when Celine and I had been dating for six months, we went on a weekend trip to Paris. We'd booked to see an opera. Some guy warbling about his life as a barber is not actually my idea of a good time, but I agreed to go for Celine's sake. The tickets cost a fortune.

Then, two hours before the opera, Celine got a call from a Polish pianist who offered to coach her in Chopin's preludes. He was over for a concert series and could only do that evening. Celine didn't even pretend to ask if I minded. I remember it was Chopin because Celine never talks about Chopin. She plays the least Chopin she can get away with. It wasn't a career capstone; it was an area of her repertoire she considered slightly lacking.

I mean in a vacuum I admire that, giving up your holiday to practice piano. But the point of us visiting Paris together, collectively –

Anyway, I went down to the hotel bar.

I drank gin. Beside me, a loud Australian woman scolded the barman for not taking Mastercard.

'What are you, Amish?' she said.

'Not my decision,' the barman said.

'Mennonite?'

'Company policy.'

'Pennsylvania Dutch?'

'Let me,' I said, and paid for her drink.

That was a decision. The rest was the path of least resistance. I listened while she talked, and followed her to bed.

Later I returned to my own room. Celine was still out. As I brushed my teeth, I composed an explanation in my head:

Hey Celine. I had tolerable intercourse
with a Mastercard holder who's fuzzy on
the distinctions between Anabaptist sects.

Some things you keep to yourself.

★ ★ ★

When I finally fucked Archie six months ago, after a decade of our being mostly platonic, we woke up in a hotel room not unlike the one I'm in now. And we made coffee.

Coffee is a ritual I've never managed to establish with Celine. When she and I moved in together two years ago, I'd envisaged a daily five minutes where I grind the beans and bring the espresso glasses to our bed. But Celine finds this sort of thing difficult to schedule because she's far too bohemian to think about time. We agreed to just do it when we both happened to wake up in unison, and of course that morning never came.

There I was, half a year after my engagement party and another six months before the ceremony, drinking coffee with Archie.

The comparison isn't fair. When I lived with Archie, I'd needed to ask him not to do coke in the sitting room, never mind show up for coffee hour.

But isn't that the point of an affair? To kid yourself it would be different with someone else?

Just long enough to escape. Then back to your real life.

★ ★ ★

172

I haven't cheated since that night with Archie. Stand-up citizen, I know. Luke for president.

But you must be wondering what happened at the engagement party.

UNTITLED 49

It's 5 a.m. now and I feel approximately like death. The room is typical for mid-priced London hotels: luxurious materials, zero space. The sheets are so soft I want to steal them, but there's maybe a half-metre margin on either side of the bed.

Our Paris hotel room will be similar if the honeymoon goes ahead.

Five hours until the wedding.

Here's what went down at the engagement party.

★ ★ ★

At 8 p.m., the hour we'd told guests to arrive at The Birches, I overheard Celine saying she couldn't find her camera. Since we hadn't invited anyone who'd been raised by wolves, this gave me plenty of time to look for it before a single person actually showed up. Celine was still talking to her uncle so I didn't announce my intention.

Which is an argument we've had many times. Her: 'Why don't you tell me when you're about to do something I didn't ask you to do?'; me: 'Because I knew you wanted it done, and why tell you it'll soon be done when I can just tell you later that I did it?'; her: 'My life strategy isn't "wait for Luke to do it", so I might have already made my own arrangements'; me: 'I can't believe you're arguing with me about your right not even to adjust the blinds, but to plan on adjusting the blinds.'

(Her life strategy is 100 per cent 'wait for Luke to do it', but anyway.)

Upstairs, I started my search with the usual question: Where would I forget to look if I were Celine?

High places and cupboards. She puts things where she can't see them, then forgets they exist. Sure enough, her camera was on a shelf in the guest room's desk, an old executive slab of a thing with a lockable door on each side.

While I was there, I checked my work email. I hadn't refreshed my inbox in several hours, which to the Americans is practically a year's vacation.

As Google's predictive text feature has improved in recent years, I've turned it into one of my games. I choose random words, let the algorithm finish my sentences, then check if this has resulted in a satisfactory email. So far: yes for pleasantries, less so for details. I let the software wish my boss a great weekend so far and great rest of weekend, and supplied the meat myself in between this bread of cheer. 'Great rest of weekend' I found especially depressing on two grounds. One: it presupposed that the other person would see your email before their own weekend was over. Two: this was apparently a frequent enough scenario that machines would now fill it in for you.

8.23 p.m. They'd be wondering where I was, and Celine still needed her camera. But first, one more email.

8.27 p.m. – someone new downstairs. From the sound of it, one of Celine's second cousins: last on guest list, first to arrive. I'd stay where I was.

175

The Birches filled with gabbing relatives, all in awe of Celine. I heard them congregate, even identified my own friends – Vivian, Archie, Shawn – and couldn't move.

If you're wondering why I surround myself with such brassy people, it's because I'm a coward on my own. I haven't become any more socially confident since my teens. I've just learned to always have a Celine or an Archie or a Vivian. Or even a Shawn.

But there I was, trapped, too nervous to emerge alone – even though they were all literally downstairs. I adore my brain, truly.

Anyway.

Someone rapped on the door.

Without waiting for a response, in walked Celine's ex Maria.

★ ★ ★

An hour later, we were in a hotel lobby. Maria talked. The speed of her articulation had smeared lipstick on her teeth, but you'd need a man braver than me to tell her.

Back in Celine's uncle's guest room, Maria had offered me two choices. I could sneak away with her and answer her questions, or she could yell downstairs that she'd found me. The first option had seemed more attractive in the guest room, since it enriched my present self at the cost of future me. I can delay gratification when it comes to work and money – but with unwanted social encounters, I invariably take the quickest win.

Now future me was current me, and I wasn't loving life.

'First question,' Maria said. 'Why are you hiding from your own engagement party?'

'Yeah, I'm not answering that,' I said. 'Drink?'

'I'll have a G&T. And you'll have one, too, like a gent.'

'Is that the custom?'

Maria nodded. 'You can't buy a lady more alcohol than you're having yourself, or you're taking advantage. Actually, I can't hold my drink at all, so you need two shots.'

I bought two G&Ts, each with only one shot, and returned to Maria in the lobby. She was elegant like Celine, but not graceful so much as staunch. Whenever Celine settled into an item of furniture, she curled up like our cat. Maria, however, crossed her legs and stretched her arms along the couch.

I claimed the armchair beside Maria and held out her drink. 'Yours, with one shot. Mine, of course, has two.'

Maria took both glass and receipt from my hand. 'Liar,' she said, scanning the bill.

'Your second question?' I said.

'You still have to answer the first.'

'Very well. I left the party because I wanted to talk to you.'

'The truth, please,' Maria said.

'More than I wanted to talk to Celine's second cousins.'

'Keep going.'

'There's also a grandaunt,' I said.

'You're threatened by Celine,' Maria said. 'You got nervous at having hundreds of people assess whether you're a good enough trophy husband.'

'Celine's many things, but I wouldn't have said rich enough to buy an entire person.'

'That kind of trophy spouse doesn't confer status at all. Not anymore. It's crass to marry someone whose sole talent is being hot. More's the pity, if you ask me, because the hot spark joy wherever they go, and ought to be nurtured like plants. But what's still acceptable is choosing someone with

177

forms of cultural capital you lack. It can easily be mutual. Celine's also a trophy for you.'

'Okay,' I said, meaning I'd had enough of the topic.

'Without you,' Maria continued, 'Celine would seem like an out-and-out headcase. Made-up job, zero social life. But with a nice stable husband, she's merely eccentric.'

'I see.'

'And Celine gives you culture. Without her, your life appears barren.'

'Fine.'

'To me, at least.'

'I gathered.'

'Now,' Maria said, 'my second question: why is Celine with you?'

'Haven't you just answered that? To your own satisfaction, at least.'

'No,' Maria said. 'I was talking social utility. On top of that, I think she's attached to you.'

'I'm blushing,' I said.

'Don't do that.'

'I was joking.'

'That, either.'

'How about I don't do anything?' I said. 'Save us both time.'

'Good boy,' Maria said. 'Want to hear my theory?'

'No, but I have the wildest hunch that I'm about to.'

'Celine likes men who are effeminately handsome, e.g. you,' Maria said, 'and women who are mannishly beautiful, e.g. your correspondent. It's the same with personality. She likes bossy women, and men who do what they're told.'

'Interesting.'

'How often do you make her come?'

'What?'

'I've shocked you,' she said with sleek relish. 'Here's my guess. 40 per cent of the time. The other sixty, you delegate to her green Japanese vibrator.'

I spilled my drink.

Maria added: 'Guess how I knew.'

Then Phoebe and Archie walked in.

UNTITLED 50

It's 7.26 a.m. now. If I'm to attend the wedding, I'd better get a move on. If I'm not showing up, I need a plan.

So let's resolve the question.

Should I marry Celine?

★ ★ ★

At Oxford people spoke about art in a way I'd never previously encountered. They didn't ask, 'Good or bad?'; they asked, 'Successful or unsuccessful?'

I liked it at first, successful or unsuccessful. It seemed less priggish, less dogmatic, than good or bad.

But artists don't set the terms on which they're judged.

The more marginalised an artist's identity, the more we assume they're trying to teach their audience a lesson. The more traumatised we believe them, the more trauma we demand they disclose. The more unaccustomed we are to seeing faces like theirs in the art world, the more crudely we compare them to the last such person who made it, even if the two artists have nothing in common stylistically or philosophically or really vis-à-vis anything that's not an accident of birth.

And we all do the same with relationships.

* * *

Traditionally, I mean.

Traditionally, we judge a couple by how closely they resemble previous couples.

Not real couples, even. Our idea of couples.

We've inherited expectations that none of us set for ourselves.

Marriage isn't good or bad, successful or unsuccessful. It just works, or doesn't. Usually doesn't, but if you're the exception then great. Jazz hands.

Now, can marriage work for me and Celine?

UNTITLED 51

8 a.m.; six hours until the wedding.

In fairness, I've passed exams with less sleep.

I've been twisting my engagement ring all night. There's an angry red indent on my skin.

Standby lights, buzzing fridge. The radiator rattles. Footfall from upstairs. My legs are restless. Stand up. Sit down. Kneel, if Catholically educated. Which I was. My mother made sure I did the sacraments – much good it did me.

Around twenty years ago, Celine and I separately rehearsed our wedding day by making our First Communion. Somewhere in South London, I wore a suit. Somewhere else in South Dublin, two years later, Celine's mother Brigid fixed her veil. Ever since those prep classes, the phrase 'Jesus died to save our sins' has bothered me. I mean even just the grammar. Shouldn't it be 'save us from our sins'? If the sins themselves were the subject of salvation, wouldn't that mean Jesus died to save your gambling addiction, i.e. to keep you gambling? Wouldn't that make him an enabler? Or Him, if you're into that sort of thing.

Also though the theology is troubling, too, at least the way it's been interpreted. The idea is meant to be that God was demonstrating his(/His) capacity to forgive. Re: collateral, one's own son(/self/Self) is persuasive – so that much checks out.

But here's what Irish culture has taken from the crucifixion: 'Suffering is inherently worthwhile. When you're in pain, you're doing something. Getting hurt is a gift to your fellow man.'

It's clear why a colonised nation would adopt a framework where misery at least served a purpose.

But when suffering is avoidable, and that parching Catholic hangover convinces you to needlessly endure pain – yeah. That's not stoicism. That's masochism, and it's a very Irish disease.

Best wrap up this speech. Or whatever it is.

★ ★ ★

Let's try a case study: our cat, Madame Esmeralda.

One and a half years ago, Celine and I got a cat. This was six months after we'd moved in together, and six months before we got engaged. Perfect midpoint.

The cat was Celine's idea. I didn't have pets growing up because our landlords never allowed them. Frankly I found the idea weird. You take a living creature away from its family, ply it with treats, and castrate it. Not sure I'd feel warmly if someone did that to me.

But Celine wanted a cat, so we got a cat. Celine named the cat. For the first two weeks, Celine did everything for the cat.

Then the novelty wore off.

Now I feed Madame Esmeralda, play with her, scoop her litter box and take her to the vet. When Celine and I are both away, I pay the students downstairs to cat-sit. Madame Esmeralda hates being alone. If you don't pay her enough attention, she rips up the toilet paper, or knocks fragile objects off shelves and marvels that this causes said items to break. She'll live for maybe twenty years. Honestly I wonder if we did the right thing. By adopting her, I mean. We chose her because she ran up to us at the shelter, so really, she chose us. Someone paid five hundred euro for a kitten, then got bored and dumped her in the park. We're lucky she was found. I get nightmares about what if she'd starved. Or what if an owl had swooped down and picked her up. And does she remember that day? Does she carry it around in her head – 'I trusted humans and they left me out to die'?

I thought I was going to say: 'my vacillation over committing to a pet shows I'm clearly not ready for marriage.' But actually all it has shown me is I'd sell my organs to keep the cat alive.

★ ★ ★

Anyway.

When it's going well with Celine – and it does go well sometimes –

When things are going well, Celine is all I see. Nothing else matters to me, not in those moments. I haven't felt that way since I was a kid.

I mean I've attempted to escape reality loads, that's literally drugs.

But that's Archie's thing. Doesn't work for me. I can be coked off my tits and the closest I get to a release is: 'I, Luke, this thing that's alive, am presently coked off my tits.' Because telling yourself, okay, time to escape reality – it's like telling yourself to forget the game. And then you've just lost the game from remembering the game.

184

But my point is.

I'm only happy when doing something that makes me forget I exist.

★ ★ ★

Incidentally, I've worked out why Celine's Uncle Grellan is so weird about me and coffee. Like 'Luke prefers coffee over tea and everyone needs to know my thoughts.'

The first time I met Grellan, three and a half years ago, I asked for coffee rather than tea. On every subsequent encounter, he did this incredibly specific thing where no one mentioned coffee in any way, and out of the blue he said:

'How much would it be you pay for your coffee beans there now Luke?'

And it's so targeted, but targeted at what? To what possible end is he asking me this question? On multiple occasions? Just, why does he care? Do you know? I don't know.

And there's definitely some string-theory-fucking-logic going on here because it's Grellan.

And I need to know.

I don't think about him for 99.99 per cent of my waking hours, but it's when he shows that iceberg-tip. Didn't need to see iceberg until I saw suggestion of iceberg, and now I need the whole iceberg or I will never again know peace.

When I say Grellan's insane, though – I mean, he's an eminently practical Irish immigrant plumber. He has never once forgot his keys or needed much effort to remember them. But, for example, I recently asked him how he ended up living in Hampstead and he said:

'All the Paddies hopped off the ferry at Euston and we ran like the Jaysus to get shot of each other, only we all went the same way, and didn't our legs give out at Kilburn. Then I thought: There's more trees in Hampstead and less Irish. There's oaks. Living things. All the pet you need, a handsome oak. And no bastúns calling you a black rabbit. So I legged it over when fiscals allowed.'

None of this is remarkable. Plenty of Irish people went to Kilburn in the eighties. Some of them got rich and moved to Hampstead. But Grellan made the story particular to him, and you'd know just from the words that he was the one telling it. I had to look up 'bastúns calling you a black rabbit':

bastún /ˈbɒsduːn/ (noun), a lout

black rabbit /ˈblæk ˈræbət/ (noun), a person who has stopped attending mass

But I enjoyed the sentence before I knew.

And that's Grellan. When I say he's a madman, I cannot point to any of his actions that seem particularly unhinged. It's more that even when he has the same bare-bones opinion anyone else would, he'll still say it in a really Grellan way.

Which explains the coffee thing.

Grellan was making, as they say, a joke.

★ ★ ★

(I promise this is relevant to whether I'll marry Celine.)

★ ★ ★

186

I always knew Grellan's joke was a joke, but I thought it was a mean joke. It's not like I earnestly thought Grellan was compiling a price index on coffee beans. I assumed he was using humour to lower my position relative to his. Except that's not how Grellan uses jokes. Grellan notices someone doing a them-thing, and he loves people, and that's why it's funny to him. Because he's like, people are a hoot. If he didn't love people the bar would be higher. He'd have to use wordplay or irony or something else to veil the aggression.

But he was teasing me about a thing I do that's funny to him. And it's not that deep.

That's what Irish dads do. They assign everyone a thing, and then they keep asking the person if they still do that thing. You could plan ahead if you wanted. If you're meeting a middle-aged Irish man and you wish to determine the content of his Irish dad joke, you could wear a yellow hat. Then every time you see him he'll go: 'Ah now what happened the yellow hat there now?'

They're showing they remembered your thing.

And they choose their things fucking randomly, don't get me wrong. There's zero overlap between what you think is your thing and what an Irish dad deems your thing.

But they're saying you matter.

I mean he obviously didn't think about it in that level of detail. There's no chance Grellan thought about it at all.

Still, that's what I mean when I say I like Grellan. He can show me how to be a man without having this destroy-or-be-destroyed thing. And once you know how to do it, it doesn't take much work. It's intrinsically rewarding, so it runs itself: being nice. I look at Grellan and on some level

I think, if I were to decide the meaning of life is happiness, and if I stopped trying to be better than people, and if I tried to love them instead – it would be an investment. I'd get to be Grellan by Grellan's age.

I once saw myself doing that with Celine.

★ ★ ★

But Celine doesn't love me just for existing.

Celine loves that I listen to her thoughts, do household things, sometimes make her come, and otherwise happily delegate the task to her green Japanese vibrator. (Or was happy to, until I learned who gave her it.)

A robot could do all that. More efficiently, re: the vibrator.

Whereas Grellan –

And not just Grellan. Archie. Archie and Grellan are two men whom I love just for existing. I've had enough presence in Archie's life that we've ended up doing stuff for each other. But that's not the point. And Grellan has done nothing for me except bring up what are by now the world's most discussed coffee beans.

Nonetheless – Grellan, weirdly, is the kind of man I want to be. I used to think I'd get there with Celine.

★ ★ ★

Used to.

★ ★ ★

Then I cheated and lied, and we got engaged, and I cheated and lied some more. Now I can barely look at her. That's not Celine's fault, obviously. But the relationship is making me worse.

Worse than what? I'm not sure. But baseline Luke can't be this bad.

★ ★ ★

Inconveniently, though, I still love her.

I'm the man I was four years ago when she stood on that stepladder. I still want her to hand me the Mozart mug. I want to feed the cat in our hideous green-and-yellow kitchenette, and to say pointless things at each tram stop. And I was lying when I said I didn't love her hands. They're my favourite part of her. They tell you who she is, what she does. Eyes, lips, the focal points of sonnets – that's sheer genetics. But her hands –

Christ, I hate this.

★ ★ ★

I still can't decide.

But there's someone I can ask.

PART V

The Guest

52

'Here's my understanding,' Vivian said.

'Yeah?'

Luke looked like he hadn't slept in forty years, including eleven that he hadn't been alive for.

Vivian picked up three raspberries from the plastic punnet, chewed them and wiped the juice from her mouth. She'd told Luke she expected to be fed, and that she hated hotel food; accordingly, he'd stepped out to Sainsbury's Local. The bed served as their table. Cocktail sausages, vegetable samosas, sushi, fruit, a one-litre green smoothie carton, all laid out on a towel – a funny sort of breakfast, but those were the best.

'Do you want the last samosa?' Vivian said.

'Go ahead.'

She took it and bit off a corner. Crispy. 'All right,' she said. 'You don't like the idea of marriage, or certainly not the kind you'd have with Celine, where all your needs and goals are sacrificed to her career. But day to day, you love the tiny intimacies.'

'Yeah.'

'Whereas Celine loves the idea of your relationship, but

she probably doesn't enjoy the actual experience.'

'Honestly true.'

'So,' Vivian said, 'you're in mutual unrequited love.'

'I didn't think that was possible – but lucky us.'

'Also, you've cheated on her multiple times, and her ex dragged you away from the engagement party – and then you lied to Celine about where you'd gone. Celine almost certainly saw you at the airport the next day, and she didn't say anything. So then you realised you're both unhappy, even if Celine won't admit it.'

'Correct.'

Vivian finished her samosa. What now? Something to drink. She poured herself a glass of the thick green smoothie, and another for Luke. 'Come on. Sustenance.'

'I can't eat,' Luke said.

'It's a smoothie.'

'I can't drink.'

'You drank coffee.'

'Which killed my appetite.'

'Suffering Christ.' Vivian walked over to the kettle. 'At least let's both have another coffee, because the point of sharing food, Luke, is to bond over joint experience.' While she spoke, she poured two sachets of instant into the mugs. 'Sugar?' she said. 'Milk?'

'Black's fine,' Luke said.

'You're sure you don't want barbarian-style?'

'Black.'

She knew very well from their housemate days that Luke only drank black, but she liked getting a rise out of him. There he was, thinking away to himself: I'm not a barbarian, I'm not a barbarian, I don't want coffee-flavoured milk. One day he'd say it aloud.

'Now,' Vivian said, once Luke had sipped his coffee, 'what are you going to do?'

Luke put down his mug. 'I'll marry her.'

★ ★ ★

The June sun was warm. It was 9 a.m.. An hour ago, after seeing Luke's text, Vivian had cycled over. She'd been visiting her parents. Their house was a two-up, two-down ex-council terrace, helmed by her father Samuel's shrubs. Back in Lagos, Samuel had been a keen home gardener. There'd been nowhere to grow things when the family first moved to Dublin, but he'd planted the garden once they found a London home.

Thirteen years later, the landlord had threatened them with yet another rent hike. Samuel recounted the exchange to Vivian while watering his flowers. 'I fail to understand,' he said, 'why this stack of bricks is worth chicken change, talk less of eighteen hundred pounds. I asked the landlord, sir, what's improved about the property of recent? No answer. None expected from madmen.'

The hydrangeas had just blossomed. They had big pastel petals and a honey-vanilla smell. 'Please could I have one for my coat?' Vivian said. 'I'm off to a wedding.'

Her father snipped a stem and placed it in her buttonhole. 'Idiot landlord. His head is not correct. Who's getting married?'

'Luke.'

Vivian's father didn't know she'd dated Luke at university, but he knew Luke as Vivian's ex-housemate.

'And who's the bride?' Samuel said.

'You don't know her,' Vivian said. And thought: Nor do I, really.

★ ★ ★

'What I worked out about you at Oxford,' Vivian told Luke on the hotel bed, 'is you want to be loved in your entirety. That's not Luke-specific. The Luke-specific thing is you treat people like shit to see if they'll still love you after.'

Luke shifted away from her, as if refusing to meet this charge head-on.

'As far as I know, Archie was your first serious relationship,' Vivian continued. 'And Archie thought you should put up with his nonsense, because that's love. Love is letting people hurt you. Archie must have learned it from someone, too. We're all taught it. But some of us get over it – and some of us terrorise the general population well into our twenties and beyond.'

Luke smiled resignedly. 'You've thought about this.'

'Not really. I'm just smarter than you.'

He couldn't contest that, either.

'It did bug me, though,' Vivian added, 'that you could profess to be into me and show it half the time, and then the other half you seemed to be actively testing my tolerance for pain. Or my tolerance for dating men, if difference there be. Anyway, I worked it out, and now I'm better at filtering applications. I spot the yes-I'll-be-needing-my-pound-of-flesh types from a hundred miles.'

'I'm glad.'

Infuriating comment in a vacuum, but she could tell from his mumble that he meant it. 'Anyhow,' she said, 'that's ancient history. Regarding the wedding.'

'Sure.'

'I would diagnose you as person-who-needs-their-pound-of-flesh, and Celine as person-who-cheerfully-denies-their-flesh-loss. I say "person" when the heterosexual paradigm is pretty transparent on who does what – but in the interest of fairness to my psycho ex-girlfriend, let's stick with "person". And it's not that Celine's some masochistic waif who longs to redeem you. She's just stubborn. If she's already decided the relationship is perfect, she doesn't give a fuck what's actually happening for either of you.'

'I mean, yeah.'

'With that being said,' Vivian added, 'you are off your literal rocker to still want to marry her.'

Luke had been twisting his engagement ring. As Vivian spoke, it slipped and fell on the bedside table. The metal clanged. It was cold and hard and gold. A circle, a line without end.

'It's too late,' Luke said. His voice was steady. 'I'm not saying she's the only person I could ever feel this way about. If you break down love – it's neural pathways. But those don't get built overnight. It takes a really long time to get addicted to someone. And it's a bitch to break the habit once it's there.'

He picked up his ring. Considered it. Placed it on his finger, over the line it had left on his skin.

Vivian collected the remains of the Sainsbury's picnic and transferred them to the fridge. 'I'm not the boss of you, thank fuck. But have you considered that she doesn't know you cheated? Dublin's small. She'll find out. And when she does, she'll be pissed. Just something to chew on. But I'm off now. I'll be back in an hour. And if you still want to marry her, all right.'

Luke didn't look convinced.

'I know you love her,' Vivian added. 'Probably she loves you, too. But you can love someone without that making them a good long-term partner. You and I love each other, right? "As friends", whatever that means. No way in hell are we ever getting married, and it doesn't make the love any less. That's why I hate "The One" – it belittles our capacity to connect. We all have hundreds of kindred spirits. Thousands, maybe. Even millions. We'll never meet most of them, but they're out there. Celine's one of yours. Doesn't mean she should be your wife.'

'I do get that theoretically.'

'But you don't feel it. Well, do what you want. I'll be back.'

53

'Vivian Nwosu: Encounters with Paintings
over 29 Years of Life'

**1. Barber, Abayomi. Year unknown. Title unknown. A
print on the wall of the Nwosus' kitchen wall, Lagos.**

Vivian is eight years old, and lives with her parents and
three brothers on Lagos Island. The family speaks English
at home, but Vivian sometimes hears her parents use Igbo
on the phone. She's top of her class, and wants to know
everything. One summer afternoon she asks her mother
about the picture hanging above the kitchen table. It's of a
stormy sea, and the sky is multicoloured. Vivian learned that
word in a book, 'multicoloured'. It means there's yellow
and orange and blue and every colour. 'Were you there on
the beach?' Vivian asks her mother. Mummy smiles and
says no, that the painting is by a famous Nigerian man.

When the family emigrates, the print is left behind.

Vivian has since asked both parents many times, and neither can recall the painter's name. She also tried her teacher
in Dublin, a smiling white woman who replied that she

didn't know much about 'ethnic' art. Vivian's best guess is that it's one of Abayomi Barber's surrealist landscapes. Some day she'll find it.

2. Uccello, Paolo. c. 1470. *The Hunt in the Forest*. Ashmolean Museum, Oxford.

Three years after emigrating again from Dublin to London, Vivian takes the train to Oxford interviews. It's early December. Her A-Level art teacher said not to get her hopes up. Ms Clarke didn't quite phrase it like that, but Vivian can interpret language. Actually, Vivian can interpret anything. Across three different education systems, the constant has been that she's smart. But what if she's not? What if the Oxford dons decide it's a pack of lies?

While checking the interview timetable in the Magdalen College common room, Vivian gets talking to the boy beside her. 'Are you a lawyer, too?' he says. Vivian is nonplussed – this maroon-scarfed seventeen-year-old does not much resemble a legal professional – but it turns out he's asking if she's applied to study law. 'No,' Vivian says, 'I'm an art historian' – she learns quickly. 'Are you on Instagram?' the boy asks, and searches her name. A notification: Archit Gupta Stopford just followed you.

After interviews, Vivian and Archie walk to Oxford's Ashmolean Museum. Vivian finds *The Hunt in the Forest*. It's a long rectangular oil painting filled with a black sky and trees and men with spears. A tribe of native warriors embroiled in primitive bloodlust, perhaps in a bid to appease their gods. But they're white, so the plaque describes technique.

Her textbook said the painting was displayed at shoulder-height. It is, if you're as tall as the curator.

3. Yiadom-Boakye, Lynette. 2010. *Any Number of Preoccupations*. Serpentine South Gallery, London.

It's September 2015 and Vivian has just moved back to London with Archie, Shawn and Luke. Two weeks after arriving, she and Luke go to a Yiadom-Boakye exhibition in Kensington. Vivian's favourite painting portrays a man in white slippers and a bright red robe. The background is dark and plain. You can't tell the subject's identity from what he owns. There's no decorated ceiling to inform you he's rich, or mismatched crockery to say he's poor. His chosen costume, his posture: that's him.

Luke wanders off. He must know Vivian wants to be alone with the painting. Many people mistake Vivian's 'I'm thinking' face for an 'I'm troubled' face, an 'I need assistance' face. But Luke never foists aid on her, and that's why he's the only person she asks. He drilled her on her flashcards before finals; he's been helping her practice for interviews, for her dream job at the Tate. He's far kinder and more reliable now than when they dated as students. That discrepancy makes Vivian sad, but more for Luke than for herself. She's all right. She has a new girlfriend now, and if it doesn't work out there'll always be someone else. She doesn't need anyone. She's enough.

4. Artist unknown. Year unknown. Title unknown. Hotel room, central London.

It's the morning of Luke's wedding.

Vivian looks at the picture above the hotel bed. Bright colours, stormy sea. Could it be –? It's not. This is corporate art, produced to match the furniture. The painting at her home in Lagos was special. Must be, or she wouldn't remember it. Yes, she brings nostalgia and biases and childhood awe to the question of whether this half-remembered print was any good. But her shoulders are shoulder-height, her universe is universal, and she makes her own mind up, and that's that.

She's had her art gallery job for nearly eight years now. The working conditions are dreadful, and recently drove the staff to strike, but Vivian likes the museum itself. Across her time there, she's had six girlfriends. Each of them found her alluringly mysterious at first – but after a certain point, they wanted to know who'd died. And they wanted her to need them, miss them; all those things Vivian not only can't express, but can't feel. So they leave. She lets them. She never chases anyone. There'll always be someone else.

She looks down from the hotel room painting now, and back at Luke. He's getting married today – unless he's not.

Vivian was mildly curious when Luke texted asking her to come over. As he describes his dilemma, she advises. She finds it cathartic to say aloud what she's thought many times: Luke's not cut out for marriage. He probably won't listen. That's all right. She doesn't blame people for being people, any more than she'd blame Luke's cat for being a cat. Anyway, it's Luke's life, not hers. Vivian doesn't take it personally when people ignore her two cents. Like Yiadom-Boakye's subjects, she won't be defined by external circumstance – whether it's objects in the background, or the actions of homo sapiens.

In any case, she's wanted elsewhere. She tells Luke she'll be back.

Then she leaves to meet Archie and Shawn.

54

Shawn was telling Vivian and Archie about the stag he'd organised as Luke's best man.

'If you wanna know what went down, I said, fuck it, lads on tour,' he said. (Although Shawn had moved to England from New York eleven years ago, he still said 'lads' as if hoping he hadn't mispronounced it.) 'Go be fucking animals. But Rakesh said, "Shawn, you're the only fucking animal here, the rest of us are civilised 29-year-olds with insomnia and lower back pain", and Tiernan said – so we –'

Shawn wasn't used to this much airtime. He seemed unsure what to do with it. Vivian had her own reasons for keeping quiet, and possibly Archie did, too.

But it wasn't like Archie to let Shawn ramble. And why had Archie missed the stag in the first place?

They sat in the back room of a Mayfair restaurant, Vivian and Archie at the banquette and Shawn on a Danish-looking chair. The interior was a mix of mid-century modern and deco. In the course of Shawn's anecdote, their pains au chocolat and mushrooms on sourdough had arrived. Vivian regretted having already filled up on the breakfast that Luke had assembled. Shawn was treating them to bottomless, so they accordingly gulped the prosecco.

'Vivian, by the way,' Archie said, 'your dress is ravishing.'

An inelegant change of subject, but she'd go along with it. Vivian held the silk to the light and showed Archie its shimmer. 'Charity shop.'

'Proper charity shop?' Archie said. 'Or Oxfam Boutique?'

'There's no flies on this one,' Vivian said.

'What?' Shawn said.

Archie seemed equally perplexed.

'Must have heard it in Ireland,' Vivian said. Such was the nature of growing up in three countries. She usually remembered to sift this or that out of her speech if she thought the other person wouldn't understand, but the prosecco was doing its job.

'Shawn,' Vivian added, 'tell us what you did for the stag.'

'We went to Scotland,' Shawn said.

'Glasgow?' Vivian said. 'Edinburgh?'

Shawn poured more prosecco for all of them. 'The Cobbler. It's a hill, and we all just fucking climbed it. Tiernan's foot hit a rock and he deadass nearly died.'

'Who's Tiernan?' Archie said.

'Luke's cousin,' Shawn said. 'I told you.'

Archie forked a mushroom from his toast. 'And I forgot, so I asked again.'

'Just shouldn't be fucking impossible to remember one guy's name,' Shawn said, 'and his one role in our lives is he's Luke's cousin.'

'Right-ho,' Archie said. 'Sincerest apologies. I'll remember Tiernan in future.'

'Bruh.'

'Will tattoo name on eyelids.'

'It's not deep.'

205

'Wrists, too.' Archie finished his toast and reached for a pastry. 'One question, though.'

'Shoot.'

'If you don't mind my asking.'

'Dude, what?'

'Who's Tiernan?'

Vivian laughed.

She'd been savouring her prosecco while the boys skirmished. To her, they were ants. The people at her gallery, too – and before that, her fellow Oxford students – and really all the world. She stood overhead and watched the little black dots: their marching lines, their tripod gait. She could live on their level. She could move among them. But she didn't have to, and often enough she didn't want to.

The persiflage of these particular two ants amused her so greatly that only at 10 a.m. did she check her phone.

Then she saw Luke's texts:

Off to meet my mother

See you at the church

PART VI

Wedding Day

55

The Birches.

McGaws present; McGaws correct. Three hours until the wedding.

Grellan was a decent worker but better yet at outsourcing. D-Day was upon them, and he hadn't a thing to do. That was as it should be. Know thyself is well and good, but more importantly, know what you're bleeding not. He settled into the armchair at the back of his study, and listened as the morning unfolded.

No sign of Celine and Phoebe's father. The absentee, true to form. The nieces would be down about that, but his sister would know what to say.

★ ★ ★

Downstairs in her brother's kitchen, Brigid unplugged the kettle. Didn't Grellan and Maggy know it was a waste leaving things on standby?

Then Brigid plugged the kettle back in again for tea. Point made. No one else was in the kitchen, but point made.

As the kettle boiled, Maggy walked down the steps. In honour of the big day, she'd swapped her usual leopard-print for zebra. Brigid would credit her sister-in-law with this much: Maggy never made any attempt to blend in with her Hampstead neighbours. The young ones in the area wore 'Scandi' shirts. The older women dressed as if they'd come from a farm, though frankly Brigid doubted they milked the cows. Many a padded jacket Brigid had seen around these parts, and from none of them extended hands that had known udder.

'Tea, Maggy?' Brigid said. The water boiled. 'It's as well you're after coming down. Two cups minimum this yoke says, and I didn't want to banjax your kettle, but it's a shame to be overfilling.'

She hoped this communicated, in a general way, that you shouldn't leave appliances plugged in.

'I'll have tea, so,' Maggy said.

Blissful ignorance. Hopeless case.

★ ★ ★

Maggy took the tea cup, and fruitlessly glared as an oblivious Brigid unplugged the now-empty kettle. Could the woman not take a hint? Maggy had mentioned to Grellan before that Brigid was always fiddling with appliances. He'd said: 'And what harm?' and Maggy had said: 'Plenty.' Grellan refused to see what was patent to Maggy: Brigid had lived in South Dublin too long, and had assimilated Protestant penny-pinching. Maggy had no objection to thrift, now, but if you asked her: Maggy, would you pay a sliver of a penny per day to not be plugging in the kettle every time you make tea? – then the answer would likely be: Yes.

The sisters-in-law drank their tea and had a pleasant conversation.

★ ★ ★

Upstairs in the entrance hall of The Birches, the photographer tested his camera. He was a cousin of Maggy's and had been hired for that reason. Nepotism, darling; c'est la vie. As he adjusted his lens in front of the preening bridesmaids, he wondered if this was quite why he'd gone to art school. The women's dresses were all mint green. It suited three of them nicely and two not at all, but he'd fix the colours later. His images would show everyone at their best, and what actual wedding could you say that for?

Now one of the bridesmaids stomped up the stairs. He switched to continuous shooting. Her real step was clunky and her pout rather smug, but he captured a split second where she seemed to be airily ascending, chin high, smooth arm on walnut bannister.

★ ★ ★

Phoebe reached the guest room. Should she knock? She did. 'It's me.'

Celine replied: 'Fuck off.'

56

Celine had broken a Waterford swan.

There were several factors involved.

★ ★ ★

First, her period started. She awoke with cramps, and on the toilet she wiped off a clot of blood. Perfect. She'd deliberately scheduled the wedding to avoid this, but the stress of planning had thrown off her cycle.

She put in a tampon and viewed herself in the mirror.

Her eyes had looked tired for months. Would the purple shadows fade when they finally said their vows?

Since last June's engagement party, Celine had stopped internally playing the piano as she went about her day. It was like losing a friend. She'd replaced the habit with headphones, but passive listening didn't offer the same companionship as the eighty-eight keys that had once resided in her brain.

As a gawky schoolgirl, she'd needed her private recitals. Mr Mac Diarmada droned about diploids; Paul Hogan threw balled paper at her neck; Leah O'Sullivan, no shyster from life's contradictions, called her both frigid and a slut. Their heads were semibreves, round and hollow. Their voices vibrated like strings. Celine stared at the desk, and played *Grand galop chromatique* without moving her hands. Partial chord on upper stave, C flat C flat – B B really, white keys – long stretch, so move lower note to left? – no, can reach on right, thank you peasant genes for large hands –

Years later Celine told Phoebe about this escape route. Phoebe replied: 'Celine, that's dissociation. You've monetised dissociation.'

But it worked. It was fun. And now she couldn't do it.

The autumn after the engagement party, she'd crunched through leaves without tapping out their crackle on her keys. In winter, the snow failed to evoke Debussy's *Des pas sur la neige*. Come spring, no Sinding's 'Rustle', no Schubert's 'Trout.' Now it was summer again, and she was still alone.

She did have Luke.

But the lie –

Not only his. Hers. The 'It's fine' lie. The 'I completely didn't see Luke at the airport after he said he was already home' lie. The 'I have no misgivings whatsoever about marrying someone who lies' lie.

But she loved him.

But he'd lied.

★ ★ ★

She returned to the guest room and texted Tanja, her old conservatoire friend and bridesmaid, with the word 'period' and several skull emojis. Tanja helpfully sent back a YouTube compilation entitled 'The Simpsons: Every Time Homer And Marge Got Married'.

Celine watched the video in bed. The first clip included casino music at the start of a drive-by ceremony. The second clip featured a few bars from Mendelssohn's wedding march, transposed to sound Simpsonsy. The third clip – which included no context as to why Homer and Marge were marrying yet again – showed an orchestra playing a longer stretch of Mendelssohn's score.

It was 8 a.m. now. She could run downstairs to the piano and play the march.

★ ★ ★

In the blue room at the front of the house, Celine lifted the lid. The piano was out of tune, but each note was exactly a semitone lower, so the gaps were the same – the instrument just had a bit of a head cold.

She liked coaxing songs out of the wonky old thing; liked knowing the keys that jammed, liked finding the touch to ease them. She'd never been able to stomach the musical sister in *Little Women*. First off, the girl was a sap. Secondly, she envied girls with nice pianos, which amounted to blaming one's tools. Any goober could tickle you pink on a supple Steinway grand. Snaggly uprights took tact, and were the real test.

After a few rounds of scales, Celine googled the sheet music on her phone and placed it horizontally on the desk above the keys.

'Wedding March' came from Mendelssohn's suite, written to accompany *A Midsummer Night's Dream*. Which was just about the most pagan play of all time – but Queen Victoria's daughter used the music at her Christian ceremony, and soon the tradition spread. And that was what Celine loved about piano. Its echoes. Its vibrations. A keyboard could take her anywhere, into any mind – from Mozart daydreaming about Turkish brothels, to Nina Simone riffing on Bach.

And there was so much more to Mendelssohn's march than the snippets played in movies.

Most performances stripped the wedding march of its episodes, playing only the famous recessional. But if you heard the whole score, the forte hit you louder and the joyous chords struck gold. It warmed you, played in full. It made you sing. That said, you could find context elsewhere. In those *Simpsons* weddings, Homer and Marge's story was the build-up. They weren't *South Park*; they weren't *Family Guy*; they actually loved each other, and those Simpsonsy bars of Mendelssohn told you so. Nothing wrong with that. Another pianistic perk: you could play your magnum opus or accompany someone else's. A sonata, yes, that was art. But a few quiet bars that helped a filmmaker say their thing – that was art, too.

Celine loved Mendelssohn and she loved *The Simpsons* and she even loved Tanja for sending her that stupid clip, and she was happy to be alive, and if fast meant happy in music notation then so be it, she'd go faster and faster and faster down the aisle –

– and the glass swan fell.

Off it flew from the piano-top.

And cracked.

57

'You did not break the swan,' Phoebe told her sister in the guest room. 'Would you get a grip of yourself? Maggy shouldn't have put it on the piano. Pianos vibrate. Any muppet'll tell you that. Besides, it's your wedding. You can break the whole house if you want.'

The Birches currently looked like this:

Guest Bedroom

- Self
- Celine

Kitchen

- Brigid
- Aunt Maggy

Red Room

- More miscellaneous relatives

Uncle Grellan's Study

- Uncle Grellan

Entrance Hall

- Bridesmaids (including Tanja, who'd probably fucked Luke)
- Photographer
- Miscellaneous relatives

Blue Room

- Piano
- One less Waterford Swan

No use, the lot of them. She'd manage on her own.

In a way, Phoebe was grateful to the crystal-cut little fucker. The broken swan was a specific, immediate thing that had gone wrong. Whereas take, for example, Tanja – she was such a tiny part of the overall picture. She was maybe number seventeen among the top twenty reasons Celine shouldn't marry Luke. With any other couple, 'The groom probably cheated with one of the bridesmaids a few years back' would be a calamitous and singular blow. But for this happy couple, on this happy day, it was utterly business-as-usual.

Let's say Tanja's number seventeen. Full list?

<u>Reasons Celine shouldn't marry Luke</u>
1. That thing at the engagement party where Luke fucked off with Celine's ex Maria

2. That same night, Luke cornering Phoebe outside the jacks and saying essentially: 'I am the shiftiest fucker on the planet but you need to trust me that everything I do is for Celine'

3. Archie not being Luke's best man anymore, or even one of Luke's groomsmen. Why? Had Luke ever explained that? Why ask your ex-boyfriend to be best man in the first place – but if you're going to ask him, why un-ask him?

4. Vivian – also an ex, also very involved in
Luke's life. Seemed too savvy to still want the
cunty bastard on a sexual level, but why all
the exes, Luke?

5. –

She could go on. The whole thing was rotten. And Celine
had seemed anxious even before swan-gate.

★ ★ ★

'We could do,' Phoebe said, '– head-the-ball. Thingumajig.
Gold dust.'

'Sorry?' Celine said.

The sisters were still in the guest bedroom at The Birches.
Phoebe sat in an antique brocade chair, and Celine stood
by the dresser. The bride already had her gloves on; the
swan's shattered glass must have spooked her about hurting
her precious hands.

'You glue it back together,' Phoebe explained. 'Then do
gold along the crack.'

'Kintsugi.'

'Swot. But I'm telling you, Maggy won't notice. Hasn't
she a million swanny yokes?'

Celine held up the broken halves. The neck and beak
were clearly a swan's. The other fragment, the back of the
wings, could have easily passed for a shell.

'There's something that's –' Celine said. 'Look, Phoebe,
just between us.'

'Got you,' Phoebe said.

Celine joined the swan halves back together and placed
them on the dresser. She was in a camisole and shorts, and

looked startlingly young. There seemed no age gap when the sisters wore pyjamas.

'I don't think Luke was telling the truth,' Celine said, 'about why he went missing at the engagement party.'

As she spoke, she looked at the floorboards.

Phoebe joined her sister by the dresser, and fidgeted with the swan – somewhat, slightly, just to line up the halves a little better. There. Hardly broken.

'If I knew something about that night,' Phoebe said, 'something that maybe – it'd change your opinion. If I knew something like that. And I could tell you. And I hadn't told you. Do you reckon you'd want to know?'

Celine took the swan again, and held it before the window.

'No,' she said, 'I'd not want to know.'

She put the swan back.

And added: 'You don't always need the full story.'

58

'It'll be fun,' Vivian told Archie.

'Right,' Archie said, and downed his espresso, 'only it won't.'

An hour and a half till the wedding.

Shawn had deserted them for best man duties. Vivian and Archie had moved on to a café with fish-patterned wallpaper, quartzite tables and Persian rugs. Once they'd sat down, Archie told Vivian he'd changed his mind about witnessing Luke's balmy nuptials.

'They're having it in the Jesuit church,' Vivian said.

'I've nothing against the Jesuits,' Archie said.

'Well, I'm not going on my own.'

'Suit yourself.'

'Let's try again. I'll say: I'm not going on my own, and you say: In that case, Vivian, allow me to escort you.'

Archie had never properly explained to Vivian why he wasn't Luke's best man anymore. Didn't have the time, he'd said – but in that case, why not just be a groomsman?

'I'm impressed they managed to book a Catholic church,' Archie said. 'Neither of them believes in it.'

Vivian laughed. 'Celine's family seem pretty good at

getting things. Remember her uncle's house?'

'But what's the appeal? Luke's bi.'

'What's that got to do with it?'

Archie didn't meet Vivian's eye, and attempted to disguise this through looking at nearby areas of her face. Vivian sensed she was close to pressing a button of some kind.

She had no idea what the button might do, which made her all the keener to press it.

Finally, Archie said: 'I don't like sophistry. And I don't like casuistry, and I don't like people lying to themselves. I hate to break it to you, but the Church is homophobic. Why marry there? I don't respect it.'

'You don't need to respect Luke,' Vivian said. 'I live beautifully without respecting Luke.'

Not in terms of his life decisions, anyway.

Interesting, too, that Archie had only mentioned Luke, when he must have known Celine was queer as well.

'Can't you see it's a cop-out?' Archie said. 'It happens to be a woman Luke's marrying, so he gets his Catholic church and the priest nods along and nobody cops that Luke might just as easily have married a man. Luke never has to ask what he'd have done. Where he'd have had the ceremony. Whether he'd have told his family: I'm not Catholic, none of you are meaningfully Catholic, I don't owe you a Catholic wedding.'

Vivian put down her coffee mug. 'That sounds to me like Luke's problem.'

Archie looked as if he had more to say. She doubted she'd get it out of him in the café.

She added: 'Shall we walk?'

221

They reached Little Venice and ambled along the canal. On either side of the water, Regency mansions and weeping willows absorbed the noise from busier streets nearby.

'I always seem to make it back to the water,' Archie said. 'This canal especially. But I think it's Irish, the water thing. When my granny used to take us out to the sea, she always said, "Are you getting in?", no context, as if the presumption is that "in" means down into the water. You're never far from the sea in Ireland.'

'Untrue,' Vivian said. 'There are fourteen landlocked Irish counties. They taught us that in fifth class. I'll never forgive my parents for waiting till my teens to leave. To think a few years earlier and I could have avoided learning where's Offaly.'

'Anyway,' Archie said, 'in Ireland "landlocked" just means you're an hour from the sea rather than thirty minutes.'

'Have you actually been to Ireland?'

'Luke and I kept saying we'd go, but we never did.'

Which brought them nicely to the real topic. 'Come to the wedding,' Vivian said. 'Luke wants you there.'

'I know,' Archie said. 'But –'

Could Archie still love Luke?

Nonsense. Vivian had moved on from Luke eight years ago. Why wouldn't Archie do the same? He had a busy job and all the illicit substances one could need. But maybe none of that was getting him over his past. Maybe it was keeping him trapped.

Perhaps she should try.

Gently as she could, she touched Archie's arm and said: 'Are you not over Luke?'

They stopped walking. Archie's face confirmed a correct guess.

'Archie.' Vivian hugged him. 'Archie, look at me. Luke is some guy with a job.'

'Okay, but I'm also some guy with a job.'

'No, you're you. So what'll we do? We can fuck off anywhere you want.'

Archie turned to Vivian with a determinedly casual smile. 'You've the wedding.'

'I was only going for entertainment. You can entertain me instead.'

'I want to go now. You know – put the full stop on it.'

Vivian sighed. 'None of you learn.'

'Learn what?'

'Let me drum this into your eejit head. The good Lord gets us over people when we get the fuck away. Cut ties. Stop dilly-dallying into their lives like a semi-neglectful godparent. Foolishness. But if you want to go' – she held out her arm – 'let's go.'

★ ★ ★

They took the Tube for a few stops, and climbed up the filthy steps into daylight.

Archie was a good person to weave through central London with. He assumed others would move for him, and they did. Groups were as fast as their slowest member, and as dauntless as their cockiest.

They crossed the road. 'Homicidal maniac,' Archie said when a taxi almost hit them.

'I hate cars,' Vivian said. She couldn't drive, and it was easier opposing it than learning.

She and Archie turned down a lane with barber shops, sushi joints and dark pubs. Then came a wider street, and a church – but no – it was Christ Scientist – theirs was further up. The pavement continued along a road of mismatched terraces. A man in a hoodie and woman in a bodycon dress approached from the opposite direction. Had they come from different venues, or was there a place where both outfits worked?

More terraces, these in a uniform line of white plaster that broke off here and there onto mews lanes. Nowadays it was a status symbol to live in a former stable. It reminded Vivian of her childhood road in Dublin, where a developer had converted a Victorian public toilet into a café. 'The menu's all right,' her father Samuel had said, 'but you wouldn't eat there, knowing.'

Archie said they were nearly there.

At the end of the road stood a grey Brutalist housing estate and a redbrick mansion block. Finally they turned to the right. They'd found the church.

59

McGaws in chaos now; McGaws asunder.

An hour until the wedding, and there'd be awful traffic to contend with.

Grellan had his principles, though it was true he invented many of them on the spot. 'Don't do things you're no bleeding use at' was one. Here was another: 'Do do things that nobody else is any bleeding use at.'

The bridal party needed to be off, and would plainly not be moving itself.

Phoebe. No tact. Efficient for that reason. She'd be downstairs from the sound of it – red room. Not what Maggy called it but forgot her word. 'Lounge,' or the like.

'It's herself,' Grellan said with some relief. His younger niece was on the sofa, staring at her phone. They did that a lot, the both of them, Celine and Phoebe, and he'd once heard it said it tampered with the brain. But they'd said that about microwaves, too, and he wouldn't be cried wolf to about the ailments of modern man.

'State of play, miss?' Grellan said.

Phoebe looked up. 'Celine's dressed. They're doing her

hair now, and then the face. Bridesmaids are grand. Maggy and Mammy are as ready as they'll ever be.'

Grellan nodded. You'd see snails shite before you saw those two ready for Celine to marry.

'It's just Dad who's not here, so,' Phoebe added.

'Does Celine want to wait for him?'

Phoebe shook her head. 'Disappointed, but not surprised, is how I'd put it.'

'Sure look.'

'She wondered could I ask you something,' Phoebe said.

'Right you are.'

'If Dad's not there, can you give her away?'

Yet again, Grellan's principles clashed. Here was something he would undoubtedly be no bleeding use at: 'ceremony (pomp and)'. But could anyone else do better?

Maggy.

Made for it, she was.

Grellan had asked her to dance all those decades ago in a Camden Irish hall. She'd stood there brokering partnerships for her friends, on no apparent authority besides knowing everyone. She'd take a youngfella's arm and link it with a youngwan's, and with a word of introduction they'd be off. Naturally the question had occurred to him whether he could be the one she kept for herself.

'Your aunt would be the one to ask,' Grellan told Phoebe. 'Her wheelhouse, so it is, giving brides away.'

'Has she experience?' Phoebe said.

'No need,' Grellan said. 'Matter of gumption.'

60

'Dapper,' Vivian told Luke. 'Perfect, gorgeous and stunning. A few queries.'

Forty minutes to go.

Luke stood with Vivian and his groomsmen in a small bright room at the back of the church. When she'd left his hotel room and he'd told her he was definitely going ahead with the ceremony, she'd texted back a reproach – 'You are actually insane' – but seemed to have forgiven him. That was Vivian for you: shocked or amused at her ant farm's locomotions, but never angry, never scared.

The others in the room were Shawn, Rakesh from work, and Luke's cousin Tiernan. Luke couldn't help feeling that Shawn's prime position should have gone to Vivian, but out of 'best' and 'man' she met only half the criteria.

In any case, Vivian had assigned herself the task of critiquing Luke's tux.

'I await your comments,' he told her.

'First note,' Vivian said.

'Yeah?'

'Would be the coffee stain.'

He couldn't believe it. His eyes hadn't left his Americano

the entire time he'd been drinking it. But there the blot was, right on his chest.

'Don't touch it,' Vivian said. 'You'll make it worse. Shawn, get vinegar, or vodka works.'

'Where?'

'Use your phone.' Before Shawn was out of eyesight, let alone earshot, Vivian added: 'There's learned helplessness and then there's can't even teach themselves that much.'

'How long have I got?' Luke said.

'I don't know. Text Celine.'

★ ★ ★

They'd be in Paris tonight. Since they'd gone there for their first big weekend away, to Luke it was the natural choice. Celine had initially responded that it felt hackneyed, a honeymoon in Paris. Luke had resisted commenting on her impulse to assume a snobbish external gaze – ugh, Paris, everyone's heard of that.

There were unsavoury associations, sure. The corniness of romanticising the French capital to begin with. Celine ditching Luke to take a Chopin class from that Polish virtuoso. Their abandoned opera tickets folded up in a leaflet, and that Australian woman Luke had approached at the bar. But Paris was also live electro at a pub near the Bastille, open-air cinema on the lawns of the Parc de la Villette, and a Group f/64 photography exhibition they'd attended in a former dance hall. Moroccan food at Au P'tit Cahoua, institution of the 13th – cream filigree screen dividers, wafting of cumin and garlic and black pepper. They'd done all that. Hadn't it meant anything?

But a memory was only as good as the brain that stored it. Celine's account would likely be: 'We went to Paris and I thought about music.' That was her experience of the world. She did X, and thought about music. She did Y, and thought about music. An accessory called Luke was sometimes there. He perhaps had an inner life, and good for him.

Vivian was right: Luke's cheating was blatant. If Celine ever cared to investigate, she'd soon find out. Just ask a bridesmaid – or ask Celine's ex Maria, even, since Maria seemed to know everything. Ask Phoebe?

Ask anyone in the bridal limo that was currently nearing the church. They'd tell Celine: leave.

★ ★ ★

Vivian returned to the groom's room, and Luke treated his shirt stain with a tissue dipped in vodka.

'Keep blotting and don't rub, do not rub, and I'll see if anyone can give you a lend,' Vivian said, and left again.

Luke's cousin Tiernan turned to him and said: 'Ah here, why don't you and me swap?'

'Kicking the can down the road, innit?' said Luke's colleague Rakesh. 'You'd need to swap, and on it goes.'

'True enough,' Tiernan said, as if rearranging his philosophy.

Rakesh got a phone call and stepped out. Shawn was still off seeking the vodka that Vivian had already found. 'Man about a horse,' Tiernan said. He slapped Luke hard on the back as he left.

★ ★ ★

Then Luke was alone.

He took off his shirt and scratched at the coffee stain.

Celine had texted saying she was ten minutes away, which meant at least twenty. Her whole family was like that. They claimed it was an Irish thing, forgetting Luke was nearly Irish and lived and worked in Ireland and had seen for himself that some Irish people arrived on time.

His bride had shown him her dress back in the Dublin flat at No. 23. It was her grandmother's from the sixties. It had those vintage T-shirt-looking sleeves, an off-white sheen, and a crochet bodice. At a distance, it resembled the cotton thing with cutouts that Celine had worn the night she'd given Luke the Mozart mug. Maybe when she walked down the aisle, he'd see her, that Celine. She'd step through the church doors, he'd turn, and there she'd be.

And closer she'd walk to him, and she'd be near – until she wasn't chemistry or chance, but an actual person.

The hair had risen on his arms. Chalky air – sediment from the walls, maybe. He twisted his ring. Paced. Twist, pace, twist, pace. Shirt stuck to his back. Sweating buckets. Christ.

His muscles were tight, as if readying him to run.

Thirty minutes left.

★ ★ ★

A knock on the door, and Vivian's voice: 'Guess who.'

'You,' Luke said.

'Guess who else.'

The door opened, revealing Archie.

61

Abba played in the bridal limousine. Celine saw the stave in her head.

'I Do, I Do, I Do, I Do, I Do'. 4/4, C major. So was Mendelssohn's march: default time, bread-and-butter key. Did all composers think marriage was milquetoast? But Abba's lyrics told another story. 'No hard feelings if we can't make it' – very Swedish. If an Irish person had written the song, it would be about bashing your head on a rock, not at anyone's request, and then cursing God that your paramour had rejected you even after you'd gone and bashed your head for them.

Americans called it a 'staff', not a 'stave' – the horizontal lines on a score. A Bostonian clarinettist had once yelled at Celine on a cruise ship where they were both playing. He'd said a) 'staves' is the plural of 'staff' when we're talking about actual sticks, and therefore b) everyone should say 'staff', not 'stave', when referring to music notation. Celine wasn't sure how a) proved b). She'd told the clarinettist that nothing he said made any sense to her, and that she didn't even say 'staves' when she meant actual sticks. She said 'staffs', probably, or would if the situation arose – which it never had so far, so maybe he was right and she'd say 'staves'. But for now, thanks to the legacy of British colonialism on Irish musical training, she'd stick with the old word: 'stave'. The clarinettist told her, fuck those guys, say 'staff'. They made little progress from there.

Why was she feeling nostalgic for that guy? Maybe she missed open conflict.

The limo was already stuck in traffic.

'How's herself?' Grellan said.

'Herself is grand,' Celine said.

Maggy hissed at the traffic. 'What are they all on the road for? Is it Every Gobshite Day?'

The limo had burgundy seats. A mirror ran along the ceiling, so you could see yourself looking up like an anxious dog. Opposite Celine were her mother, aunt and uncle. The bridesmaids sat by her side: Phoebe, Tanja, and another conservatoire friend, Ró, the one whose boyfriend Maria had gossiped about. Luke didn't do that, at least – conduct veiled psychic warfare against his entire social circle. He only did it to her. He sure made a girl feel special.

Luke, Luke, Luke.

Although the limo was warm, Celine shivered in her cap-sleeved gown.

In her beaded white purse were the two broken swan halves. At Phoebe's politic suggestion, Celine had informed Maggy of the accident only once they were in the limousine. Surrounded by family in a luxurious setting, Maggy had laughed it off: 'Sure consider it a wedding gift. A half for him, and a half for yourself. Mind you don't cut your finger, but.' Then Phoebe asked which of them got the arse, and any residual wrath in Maggy had travelled Phoebe-wards.

The bridal purse still lay in Celine's lap. She'd wrapped each half swan in a sock to protect her hands, and wore satin gloves for good measure.

The glass couldn't hurt her.

But Luke could.

62

Vivian had closed the door on Luke and gone to look for Archie.

Twenty minutes until the ceremony began.

Her ant farm was filling up.

She'd met a few of Luke's family members at last year's engagement party. There they were on his side of the church. His mother looked like a fifty-year-old Celine. Same square face, same muted clothes, same coiffured need for control. They justified their drabness, these monochrome women, by claiming it saved them decisions. Nonsense. If 'Red or blue?' could give you a nervous breakdown, you'd probably still have one in beige.

She spied Shawn entering the church. Was he heading back to the groom's room? But he got detained every few pews by university friends.

They'd been popular, the four of them, at Magdalen. She could tell from today's turnout. Hadn't realised it at the time, because they were happy in their self-contained bubble. There'd been things she couldn't discuss with the boys – not even Archie, who was taken for Greek as often as Indian, and was stopped less often by the porters. 'Closed to visitors.' She'd tried wearing houndstooth blazers and brown Oxfords – how do I spell it out to you muttonheads that I go here, I know, I'll wear shoes with the same name as the bloody university – and those men continued to stop her, so then she wore whatever she wanted.

She'd learned by that point that she couldn't fix people. All she needed to know, really, in any human transaction, was whether it was right for her; whether it fit. That was why she'd dumped Luke when they were twenty. 'Why doesn't he text?' was none of her business. The fact was, he didn't text, and she wanted someone who did.

Shawn met her in the aisle. He gave her a high-five. 'Can you go tell Luke it's almost time?'

'I'm just looking for Archie,' Vivian said.

'Why?'

'Luke's shirt.'

'Oh, yeah. Shit. I forgot to buy vinegar.'

There was no sign of Archie on Luke's side of the church, so Vivian scanned Celine's.

The main McGaw family members hadn't arrived yet; they'd be coming with the bride. But the grandaunts were there in their tweeds, and the younger relatives had their big Irish heads on them. You could tell Irish-Irish white people from diaspora Irish white people because the diaspora didn't wear orange foundation, except if they were Fiat 500 diaspora and then they wore more. As for the lads, the Irish-Irish ones had more acne, or appeared to because they were paler.

Vivian wasn't as invested in these differences as Archie, but it tickled her to classify her ants.

And there Archie was, near the back.

Vivian waved. 'Archie,' she mouthed. 'Come.'

Luke needed a shirt. Both boys needed to talk. And if the ant farm caught fire, she'd get to watch.

63

They had fifteen minutes to get Celine to the church.

To Phoebe, the limo's back compartment looked like this:

<u>Front seats behind driver</u>
Brigid – Grellan – Maggy
<u>Back seats</u>
Celine – [self] – Ró – Tanja

'Is this the road?' Aunt Maggy said.

'It is,' Brigid said.

'The road to the church?' Maggy said.

Grellan said: 'So says Maps.'

'Is Maps I'm after asking?' Maggy said. 'Or is it the eyes in your head?'

'The eyes asked Maps, and Maps says it's the road,' Grellan said.

'If it's not the road we'll be late,' Maggy said.

Phoebe said: 'We're late anyway.'

'More late,' Maggy said.

'What's the music for the ceremony?' Ró said.

Bridesmaid who hadn't fucked Luke. That was how

Phoebe remembered who Ró was. If that didn't tell you everything you needed to know about Luke –

From her window seat in the limousine, Celine said: 'Nothing outlandish. Mendelssohn.'

'Ah,' Ró said. She seemed not to want to be rude.

'A bit clichéd, or?' said Tanja, who had never in her life faced such a compunction.

'It's only clichéd if you're boring,' Celine said. 'If you can't think new thoughts about old things. There's plenty of complexity in the score. And it means something to people who don't know composers. It means something to Luke.'

'That's nice,' Ró said.

There wasn't much one could say to that, so they all stopped talking.

The conversation of their elders once again became audible from the other side of the limo. 'Religion's like kids,' Uncle Grellan was saying. 'If you've a new one it's all you'll talk about, but you only want to hear about your own.'

'Unless you're Catholic, and then hearing about your own's worst of all,' Brigid said.

Phoebe piped up. 'Your heads are in Ireland,' she told her mother and uncle. 'Catholicism's sexy in England. It's the first thing you tell people, if you're Catholic.'

'It is not,' Aunt Maggy said. 'I've been in this country forty years, miss. Do you know who I've told I'm Catholic?'

'Your priest,' Phoebe said.

'I told my hairdresser last year,' Maggy said. 'It was Ash Wednesday, and hadn't I the ashes on my forehead, and she asked was it a charcoal peel.'

'Well, was it?' Phoebe said.

238

'That's all,' Maggy said. 'Not a soul besides the hairdresser, who's gifted, mind you. Dependent on the woman so I am. Not a soul besides her have I ever told I'm Catholic.'

'You're missing out,' Phoebe said.

Maggy was about to retort, then saw something. 'It's the road,' she said, and screamed. 'The church! Look, it's the church –'

64

Vivian showed Archie to the groom's room, and led him in to swap shirts with Luke.

'I'll preserve your modesty,' she said, and closed the door. And stood outside, and waited.

65

Luke and Archie said nothing for a while.

Finally Archie spoke. 'I might – I think you'd better borrow someone else's shirt.'

'Wait,' Luke said. 'I'm glad you came.'

'Vivian roped me into it.'

'Archie,' Luke said, 'can we talk?'

'What, now?'

'Yeah.'

'Right, but,' Archie said, and paused – 'aren't you getting married?'

'About that,' Luke said. Once Archie plainly wouldn't be responding, Luke continued: 'I'm not sure.'

Archie still said nothing.

'About getting married,' Luke said.

'Well,' Archie said, 'according to the schedule, you've got ten minutes to make your mind up. But I'd imagine Celine will be at least another five.'

Luke laughed.

More silence, and eventually Luke said: 'I haven't been upfront.'

'Haven't you?' Archie said.

'No. When I say I'm not sure – I mean, I'll only explain if you want.'

Archie said: 'I think you're the bigger "if" here.'

'Fair.' The bonhomie in Luke's voice sounded forced. 'Honestly I'm not great at knowing what I want.'

Archie gave a sharp laugh. 'I'll have to disagree with you there, old brick. I've spent a long time in denial. But it's always been gloriously, manifestly observable what you wanted. You want what we've been doing up until now. You told me as much ten years ago. I should have listened.'

'I'm sorry.'

'Only because you're finally having to decide.'

Now Luke could no longer contain his panic. 'But if we didn't have to choose –'

'Too late. Where I was a few months ago, or even a few weeks ago – you could have met me there. Even this morning, you could have had me. But nobody stands still forever. Maybe one day you'll learn that everyone else is just as interesting as you, or maybe you won't. I don't care.'

'Archie. Tell me and I'll –'

'Don't.'

'I'll not waste your time promising I'll change,' Luke said. 'You can't believe me. I don't expect you to. But if –'

'You might change,' Archie said. 'I wouldn't bet money on it, so I'm not going to bet my life.'

Luke said nothing at first. Then: 'I did tell you.'

'What?' Archie said.

'Nothing.'

'Repeat to me what you said.'

'It's – I did tell you I'm not good with relationships.'

'See, Luke,' Archie said, 'the idea of you, I loved. He was an idiot, but he cared. You? You're nothing. You don't mind if I'm hurt. You just mind being blamed. So in deference to your wishes, I'll think of you as a tapeworm. The tapeworm did nothing wrong. The tapeworm can't conceive of wrong. But if a tapeworm kept fucking me over, I'd get rid of it.'

Archie left through the interior door. It slammed.

★ ★ ★

Or it didn't.

Luke and Archie said nothing for a while.

Finally Archie spoke. 'I might – I think you'd better borrow someone else's shirt.'

'Wait,' Luke said. 'I just wanted to say thanks for coming.'

'You're welcome,' Archie said. 'That sounded curt. I do mean it. Sometimes I wish – no, wished – but anyway, it's not important. Strange, you getting married. But I'll get used to it.'

'There's something Celine once told me,' Luke said, 'about every relationship needing a harmony and a melody, and you can't just have melody.' He spoke as if recalling what he'd already explained to himself. 'And something else about – honestly, I'm not sure she agrees with me on this, but commitment isn't something you can just will yourself into. Like piano. It takes hard work, and that bit you choose. But you also have to want it, and it's not your fault if you don't.'

'Quite – only I'm not sure why you're so keen to convince me,' Archie said, not unkindly.

'I mean, fair,' Luke said. 'It's something I've been – you know. Whether we've got – Celine hates this word, but – the talent to make it work. Anyway, we'll find out. That's all anyone can expect from marriage. Finding out.'

'She's nearly here,' Archie said. 'Chop-chop.'

A pause, during which the men presumably changed shirts.

Then Luke stepped out into the church.

★ ★ ★

Or he didn't.

The first outcome was possible. So was the second.

But with her ear close to the door – not against; she did have standards; but near – Vivian heard the following.

Luke and Archie said nothing for a while.

Finally Archie spoke. 'I might – I think you'd better borrow someone else's shirt.'

'Wait,' Luke said – and his phone rang.

Three rings.

Then Luke told Archie: 'It's Celine. You might want –'

'Roger.'

Archie left and closed the door behind him. When he saw Vivian, he raised his eyebrows. Vivian smiled back at him from one side of her mouth. They stayed there in silence outside the groom's room.

Luke's phone was ringing through the wall.

They heard a pause –

Then: 'Celine?'

66

They'd reached the church, five minutes late.

Etta James's 'At Last' played as the limousine pulled in, but Celine still had Abba in her head. Textured vocals, saxophone riff. No hard feelings if we can't make it.

If only it were that easy.

The bridal party left the car, but Celine stayed sitting.

Tanja had brought confetti and party horns. She shared her supplies with the group outside. Everyone screamed and laughed, and the photographer snapped them in one long burst. He held down the button and his clicks went off like bullets. Snap snap snap over Etta James, and the limousine harboured the residual tang of countless women's perfumes. How many other brides had been in this car? And where were they now? Still married?

Party horns, laugh, click, horn, laugh, click, and she wanted this – she did –

– but she was wretched from the lies.

Luke was waiting in the church, and it was too late, and she had to marry him now.

All year, there'd been a tightness in Celine's chest. It was the same way she'd stiffened when Maria had wanted her to lie. She'd suppressed her rage for Luke, had squashed it as small as she could – but now – to stand in front of everyone they knew and pretend once again –

It would be the greatest lie she'd ever told, and to the largest audience.

And the rest of her life would proceed from that lie.

It was one thing to glue a shattered object back together. To brush away the sharp fragments, wipe the edges clean, secure the border with glue, and paint gold dust on top. There was no pretence, then, that the thing hadn't fallen; everyone knew you'd picked it back up. Celine would muster far more mendacity today when she marched down the aisle. She'd grip two halves, call them whole, and ignore that they might make her bleed.

She clasped her fingers around her purse, around the broken swan.

'Would you hurry, Celine.' Phoebe stuck her head back into the limo. 'The crowd expects.'

'Just a minute,' Celine said.

'Move.'

'No.'

'Wedding.'

'No.'

'Wedding wedding wedding.'

'Phoebe, for the love of God' – and Celine touched the purse again, and beckoned her sister into the car.

'Celine,' Phoebe said, 'what's the craic?'

'Nothing.'

'Come on.'

'Nothing,' Celine said. 'Just – I want to know.'

'You what?'

246

'When you asked me before – I've changed my mind. I want to know.'

So Phoebe told her.

Chords sounded from the church – the organist was warming up. Camera clicked, horns blared, confetti flew. Green bridesmaid dresses billowed. Grellan and Brigid wiped their eyes; Maggy held out the tissues she'd fortuitously packed. And the sisters huddled in the car, and Phoebe held Celine's hand, and Celine held her purse which in turn held shattered glass.

'You go out and explain,' Celine told Phoebe.

Then Celine picked up her phone.

67

'Celine?'

　'Luke.'

　'I –'

　–.

　'Celine?'

　'I'm here, Luke.'

　'Say something.'

　–.

　'Celine.'

　'Luke – I can't.'

68

8 p.m., rooftop restaurant, twenty storeys high.

★ ★ ★

'Shots,' Maria decreed. Her flock obeyed.

Tanja, Gráinne, Ró, Jack: all the conservatoire friends besides Celine. Understandable in the circumstances, and at least Celine was paying for the drinks. Or her family were, more like. No way could Celine cover an open bar for 150 people in central London. Celine, unlike Maria, had yet to win an international piano prize. Celine, unlike Maria, had no Deutsche Grammophon record deal. Celine, unlike Maria, lacked a massive YouTube following. And Celine, unlike Maria, had been the first of the two to establish another long-term relationship – which had now gone majestically tits-up. Poor Celine.

Five tequila shots arrived with salt and lime.

Maybe Maria drank to celebrate her triumph. Or maybe Maria drank because despite all her successes, she was still lurking at her ex's cancelled wedding. Either way, the tequila was fruity.

'Would you watch yourself?' Maria said.

Luke's best man had bumped into her. Shane? Seamus?

The best man gave no response. He was trying to ditch the photographer.

★ ★ ★

'Read the room,' Shawn said.

The photographer gaped through his lens. 'Give me more.'

'Dude, I wasn't giving you any,' Shawn said.

'You hate me, darling,' – still staring into his lens. 'Sweetheart, you despise me. Ah – but there – is that a smile? Hold it for me, pet.'

Shawn surrendered to being photographed. It was those goddamn corporate headshots all over again. And the worst thing about these jerks – you ask him? – was they treated you like a lunkheaded kid. Ickle Shawn doesn't wanna smile? No, asshole. Shawn's got other fish sizzling in his wok. In his skillet, or whateverthefuck.

He couldn't cook for shit, but he could tell you this much: they'd saved the day.

He and Celine's Aunt Maggy.

An hour ago, at the church, Maggy had beckoned at Shawn while the organist was warming up. 'You've heard they're after calling it off?' Maggy said, and when Shawn said no, she whispered a few sentences in his ear. Balls. But then Maggy added: 'Reception's paid for anyway, so we'll shuffle them that way. I'll do bride's side, you do groom's.' Easy from there. Open bar; move it, pricks. Some of them were like, Shawn, what the fuck? But he'd said: 'I'll explain later, come on, man,' and then they all left the church and arrived at the restaurant and he still refused to answer any questions. Give them nothing. That's how you nail best man.

After escaping the photographer, Shawn found his fellow

groomsmen, Rakesh and Tiernan, on two velvet armchairs in the corner.

'You ask me,' Shawn told the other men without pre-amble, 'I mean you wanna know my stance – love is diapers.'

Rakesh looked at his phone, and Tiernan scratched his head.

Shawn continued unperturbed. 'Affection's, you like them. Love's, you'll change their diapers. If necessary. You get me?'

'No,' Rakesh said, 'not quite.'

'What I'm saying,' Shawn said – one had to be patient – 'is before you have a kid, you need to ask yourself: will I change this kid's diapers? And not just in infancy. If a bus hits them when they're twelve and they can't move their arms and they're incontinent for the rest of their life, will I change their diapers? You gotta ask that. And if you can't answer "yes", don't have a kid.'

'Ah now,' Tiernan said.

'Same with pets. I told Luke when he and Celine got that cat. I said, when kitty gets old, she might start shitting on the floor. You'll have to clean that, or you'll have to put her in diapers. If you can't deal with that, don't get a cat.'

'And Luke ignored your sage advice?' Rakesh said.

'You wanna know what I think, I think he'll change kitty's diapers, but he won't be happy about it. No way Celine'll change them. So Luke should take the cat. But dudes, guys, my compatriots, here's what I'm saying. If you tell someone you'll be with them forever, you gotta mean you'd change their diapers.'

'C'mere,' Tiernan said, 'was this your best man's speech?'

'Yeah, yeah – dickheads. But if you're looking for my take – there are many possible life events that could put your spouse in diapers. And if you wouldn't change their diapers, doesn't mean you're a bad person necessarily. But don't marry them. That's why I don't fuck with relationships.'

'Because,' – Rakesh spoke slowly, as if offering Shawn extra time to furnish a better argument – 'because when you hit it off with someone, you start having intrusive thoughts about potentially changing their nappies.'

'Yeah, man. Wait – he's back. Camera prick.' Shawn gave the photographer the finger.

★ ★ ★

The photographer heeded Shawn's gesture, and made himself scarce.

Scanned the crowd.

From patriarch to mammothrept, all were off their tits.

No literal children, thank God. Nightmare to photograph. No appreciation of angles.

Now, zoom out. Capture the venue before the sun sets. Walls and ceiling of glass. Look out: Hyde Park, Kensington High Street, mansion blocks, terraces – or, if you prefer, Mayfair and skyscrapers and the Thames. Lovely, lovely, lovely. Snap.

Opposite the bar was a dance floor. Thirty-or-so attendees had already migrated there. Beautiful. Snap, snap, snap. Others sat on the long wooden benches, their elbows arranged around empty plates and a half-eaten five-tier cake. A larger pack of guests stalked the bar. Peripatetics strolled to and from the toilets – What did women do in there? Lay eggs? – or stood by the window, swooning at the sights. They looked almost poetical. Snap.

The photographer awaited further instruction from his muse.

None came, so he looked for Grellan.

There he was – near the cake, shouting.

Zoom in.

Snap.

★ ★ ★

McGaws ate and drank, emphasis on 'drank'.

All present, all correct.

Grellan himself, Maggy naturally, Brigid, Phoebe, Grandaunt Bernadette, and the young one Sorcha of Flann's. Even Flann himself – Grellan's brother – was there in the corner, regaling Luke's Oxford chums with his lore on cattle sales. Flann's advice wasn't worth the fell it stood up in, something Flann and his advice had in common – but them galoots and go-boys were easily taken in. The big blathering bhéal on him. 'C'mere till I tell yiz the going rate for heifers.' Flann didn't know the going rate for arse versus elbow, but let the poor daw have his day.

Celine?

Grellan had seen his niece earlier at the reception. She still wore her dress, and had headed straight for the bar. A true McGaw: alcohol the last stop on any flowchart. Possibly she was still drinking in the corner. The ambient huddle had grown big enough to hide her.

A decent hooley, considering. And mostly Maggy's doing.

'It's a blinder you're after pulling,' Grellan yelled to Maggy from across the bench.

The cake stood between them, a peony-iced monster. When Maggy had cut it an hour ago, she'd plucked off the wedding figurines and dumped them on a side plate. She'd hovered her knife over the Luke-doll for a wee while, but spared him in the end; the Lord would decide his fate, or else the cleaners.

'What are you after telling me?' Maggy shouted back at Grellan.

'You did well unmaking a hames.'

'Of today?' Maggy said. 'Sure no hames was made.'

'I'd be speaking generally,' Grellan said, 'but the usual thing before a reception would be to have a wedding.'

'Ah now,' Maggy said. 'Gin on the house and no priesting. There's hard sells and there's piss-easy.'

'By-the-by, have you seen Celine?'

'I haven't. Your sister might've' – pointing at Brigid.

★ ★ ★

From the dance floor, Brigid caught Grellan's eye. She smiled, and extended her grin to Maggy, family saviour. The second-best time for that wagon to start minding her own business was decades ago, and the best time was never.

Brigid's youngest, Phoebe, was in heated negotiations with the DJ. They stood at the turntables and fought like Kilkenny cats.

'Play Mitski,' Phoebe shouted.

'Mitski's not wedding music,' the DJ yelled back.

'Wedding's cancelled.'

'But –'

'Play Mitski.'

A compromise was struck: they settled on 'Washing Machine Heart', which sounded upbeat. Then Brigid listened properly to the lyrics. Another of what Phoebe called her sad girl songs, about the speaker entering a relationship that she knows will break her. It never changed, did it? No matter how far women advanced in legal or institutional or whatever-you-want-to-call-it equality, the young ones still proffered their hearts in cupped hands, so that any aul vulture could lunge. Brigid had done it thirty years ago.

Her ex-husband had seen himself as a complicated man. If the ailment were hers, Brigid would have asked: what complications, and how to simplify? But for him, it was enough to tilt his head and hear a clack.

At least Phoebe only dated women, though they might have been bad ones for all Brigid knew. An independent girleen altogether, her youngest – maybe too independent, in that sad little room in London. But as the Mitski song faded away, Phoebe swayed contentedly. She was a great one for the dancing. A pity the ballet never took.

Phoebe safe. But Celine?

Brigid scanned for a puff of white. Wasn't she after seeing Celine not an hour ago? Somewhere at the bar, if memory served.

No sight.

Then a waddle of suits split off. Celine had been behind them, perched on the backmost stool.

Chatting to your man. Luke's friend.

69

'I'm a cretin,' Archie said.

'If you call yourself a cretin you're calling me one,' Celine said. 'And I'm not a cretin.'

'I spent ten years doing boyfriend things without being his boyfriend.'

'You were being his boyfriend. He just wasn't being yours.'

'What happened to not calling me a cretin?'

After her phone call with Luke, Celine had left the church alone to buy vodka in Tesco Express. Then she'd kept walking along the road. A policeman had narrowed his eyes at her as she swigged from the bottle, but he'd said nothing. How must she have looked to him? Wedding dress, Smirnoff, no man. As it should be.

After a nice long stroll, she'd joined the reception. Phoebe had met her at the door and piloted her through to the bar, fending off enquiries.

Then Celine sat and drank alone. She left her bridal purse on the stool beside her, and nobody dared ask to sit there for some time. Finally Archie did. But she hadn't objected. There were worse people.

They'd been talking for hours now, and were still on the topic of Luke.

'Part of me thinks I can make him commit,' Archie said.

Celine sipped water. 'You can't, and if you could then you wouldn't.'

'Between us we've workshopped the whole thing. Sorry, by the way.'

'What for? You don't owe me anything.'

'Now you're sounding like him,' Archie said.

'Have my completely unnecessary apology in return, so. I didn't get engaged to Luke with the chief aim of hurting you, but I'd say it hurt.'

'Vivian said something. Let me remember. It was – Luke's just some guy with a job.'

'We're lab rats. You give us anxiety over something and we conclude it must be worth having.'

Archie flagged the barman while maintaining eye contact with Celine. 'I'm going to go and sleep with the worst man ever, and it will still be less pathetic than fighting anyone over Luke.'

'I'm never fighting anyone over a man,' Celine said. 'If he can't decide, he's all theirs.'

'I've been just as bad as Luke, really.' The barman came over. Archie ordered a Black Manhattan, then turned back to Celine. 'I've been frightful to everyone but Luke. And also to Luke.'

'Well, now you know not to be,' Celine said.

'I doubt you'd be quite so magnanimous if you were one of the people in question.'

'Oh, I'd want you dead. But everyone's somebody's villain.'

'We don't all cause the same amount of harm,' Archie said.

'I know. But let's take Mother Theresa. A low-harm individual, I'd say. Still, if I'm on a train with Mother Theresa and she coughs on me, then in my story she's the cougher.'

'Haven't they canonised her? Saint Theresa now.'

'Archie, until I explicitly request more Catholicism, please assume I'm full.'

★ ★ ★

They kept talking. Archie downed two shots back-to-back. Celine's vodka from earlier was wearing off, so she ordered iced tea with a double shot of rum.

'By Jove, I've been banging on,' Archie said. 'How are you?'

'Do me a favour, Archie,' Celine said – 'Don't ask.'

She'd need to process the cancelled wedding in her own time. But that was a beastly word – 'process'. As if memories were pig flesh. As if you dumped your experiences into a grinder, then packaged the output and labelled it. Couldn't you leave things? Let them settle into you, without knowing what to call them? People asked how-are-you, and expected a quick answer. So she played pretend. She said fine, or not fine, or whatever they wanted to hear. But for herself – for living with herself – for taking an interest in herself, even when her feelings were as maddeningly opaque to her as they were to anyone else – she needed to sit with ambiguity. It was hard, but lying was harder.

For now, Celine changed the subject back to Archie. 'I feel like there's something you wanted to ask me,' she said. 'But you're worried you'll lose face. You're like him that way. So I'll answer, and if it wasn't the question, I'll cope.

Here you go: I don't think he loved you any less. Actually his devotion to you is obvious.'

Archie tipped his shot glass for dregs.

Celine continued: 'Probably he told you he didn't want a relationship, and you did what sane people do, which is say you don't want one either.'

'No,' Archie said, and flagged the barman yet again, 'it was plain what I wanted.'

'What did you say?'

'It was so long ago. Bloody hell. We'd just finished our first year at uni. I said I can't believe you're fucking off to Ireland for three months without warning me, and he said I told you I'm like this so what do you expect, and I said I couldn't do it anymore. Then I went and did it for ten years.'

'That's all you said?'

'What else was there to say?'

'He wanted you to contradict him,' Celine said. 'And you can't do it by scolding. So that would be why he shut you down. If you'd said, "Luke, I want us to be together, and if we can't then we need to break it off completely or I'll be tortured with false hope" – I think that's what he was after. He needs the ultimatum.'

'He's a child.'

'You were both kind of young.'

Archie fiddled with his little white pocket square. 'Joke's on me, because I still wish I'd said it.'

'You couldn't have known. And I did say it, and you've seen how that turned out.'

The barman came over. Before Archie could say anything, Celine asked for a ramekin of peanuts. 'Drink as much as you want,' she said, 'I'm not your mother – but this way it won't hit your bloodstream quite so fast. Also,' – the barman had left to get the peanuts – 'I don't think you were ready either. If you can't say you love someone until you're sure they'll say it back –'

'Like you said, we were children,' Archie said. 'But if he and I – if we both got over ourselves a bit – and if we turned into proper adults and not just toddlers who've been put through some sort of medieval stretching device. Do you think maybe then –?'

'I've heard great things about the healing properties of time.'

'I ruined his wedding.'

'Don't flatter yourself,' Celine said. 'We ruined our own wedding. Mainly by having one.'

'Nearly having one.'

'Could you be more pedantic?'

'I'm just saying,' Archie said.

'And I'm just asking,' Celine said. 'Can you be more pedantic? Within the scope of your potential, is there a latent level of pedantry that you haven't yet attained?'

'I'm a lawyer,' Archie said. 'So no.'

Their peanuts arrived.

Luke had been right about one thing: Celine was warming to Archie after all. She didn't do enough of that, did she? Enjoy people.

She'd been a vain little idiot before, thinking her brilliance uniquely prevented her from being understood. Nobody knew anyone, not fully. Her loneliness wasn't special. Pick a human – any human – anyone you know: we've all felt there's too much of us for a fellow individual to comprehend. That's why you need people, plural: so that between them, they'll understand all of you. From now on, she'd stop asking one partner to give her everything. Someone could share her love of piano, and someone else could commiserate over being the eldest daughter in an Irish family, and someone else could find the best way to breathe into her ear – yes – just so, and someone else could get her past the whole debacle with Luke.

Celine would be in Paris soon with a hotel bed to herself. In the lobby was a grand piano the manager had said she could play. Maybe she'd practice, maybe not. Her time would be all hers. Americans liked Celine because she wanted their approval, and the French liked Luke because he didn't. She could be both of them now, and hate everyone and love anyone, and she'd see how she acted on her own. She'd wear cropped jeans, a white shirt and a trench coat: what you wore to be safe. For her it would be a risk. They'd never know.

70

'Vivian, my oldest friend,' Phoebe said, 'would you have a smoke?'

'Several,' Vivian said – 'all for me.'

'I bought a pack this morning,' Phoebe lied. 'Then today happened.'

Vivian gave a half-smile and handed Phoebe a cigarette.

They stood at a side entrance to the restaurant. Phoebe was still in her mint green bridesmaid's dress, and Vivian wore orange.

'How's Celine?' Vivian said. 'I saw her with Archie.'

'She'll survive,' Phoebe said. 'She's grand with real things. It's ideas that trip her up.'

'Luke's the same. I suppose that explains it.'

'That they nearly got married, or that they didn't?'

'Both,' Vivian said.

They finished their cigarettes. Vivian offered Phoebe another, which Phoebe accepted. No amount of nicotine could age her faster than spending a whole day with her family.

'You'd know more about Celine, evidently,' Vivian said, 'but Luke's problem is he can't talk to people. It took me years to realise I'm probably his closest friend.'

'He was close to Celine for a while,' Phoebe said. 'And Archie.'

'Sure,' Vivian said. 'But he can't talk to Celine about Celine, and he can't talk to Archie about Archie, and God knows he can't talk to one about the other.'

'And he doesn't see that as a problem.' Phoebe took a drag of her cigarette. 'Repressing everything. He thinks he's doing people a favour.'

'Their martyr complexes had a mutually enriching relationship. I just hope the rest of them will be all right.'

'I don't think Celine has a martyr complex. She hates conflict, but only because it's hassle.'

'Really?' Vivian said. 'Maybe I read that into her.'

'The longer I'm alive, the more I think you can tell fuck-all about a person from what someone else says about them.'

'But you can tell plenty about the person saying it,' Vivian said. 'You know, you handled today quite well.'

'Did I?' Phoebe said. 'I envied you. Not getting involved.'

'I don't tend to. Sometimes I think I should.'

'Not with Luke. Promise me not with Luke.'

Vivian laughed. 'Luke should get involved with Luke. He's spent decades putting that one off.' She stubbed her cigarette. 'Unless I'm really saying that about me.'

'Did we ever decide who was right about talent?' Luke said.

Celine sidestepped a stone on the dirt path. 'I think we both were. Nobody's automatically good at anything. But to practice a skill, you need dopamine. You physically can't pay attention without it. So if my endocrine system rewards me for playing music, and yours doesn't – well, it's no wonder I'm better.'

Luke hadn't meant the question so literally. But that was Celine for you: zero subtext.

They'd met at the Hyde Park entrance off Upper Brook Street. Celine had arrived in her wedding dress. Luke was still in his suit as well, and strangers gave them encouraging smiles as they walked across the grounds.

'We need to decide things,' Celine added.

'Things?'

'Flat. Cat.'

'Okay,' Luke said, 'so since you're taking the honeymoon, I should probably go back to No. 23 and move my things out. And I'll take Madame Esmeralda with me.'

'Thank God,' Celine said. 'I love her, but she'd die.'

'If she stayed with you?'

'Yes.'

'Honestly true.'

'Shut up,' she said.

It was the most relaxed he'd felt around her in well over a year.

Celine added: 'You keep the flat, though.'

'I mean,' Luke said, 'this is all my fault.'

'I left you.'

'Because of shit I've done.'

'I didn't want to get married,' Celine said. 'The shit you've done just forced the issue.'

'Really, you take the flat.'

'I can't afford the rent on my own.'

'Nor can I.' Luke would miss the sash windows, stone steps and red door, and even the flimsy floorboards and peeling paint. The history –

But the money wasn't there.

'Fine.' Celine was brisk. 'The flat is an albatross. We both contributed to this mess, but your contribution was greater, so you get us out of the lease. However, I was also at fault, so I'll keep paying my half of the rent until you've sorted it.'

'Where will you stay?'

'With Brigid.'

Ah, yes – the spacious childhood home, the family who softened every fall. He stopped feeling guilty, and agreed to the arrangement.

'Oh, and return the gifts,' Celine said. 'Write notes.'

They'd reached the Serpentine Bridge in the park. The river flowed under five arches of honey-coloured stone. Tourists thronged along the parapet while cyclists raced past. Children screamed, licked ice creams, chased dogs. The sky was clear.

Celine leaned towards the water, exhaled slowly, and held out a white purse in her satin-gloved hands. 'This is silly, but.'

'But what?' Luke said.

'Did I tell you I dropped a swan?'

'You didn't.'

He'd picked that up from her: 'You didn't' rather than 'No'. What would he do with these Irishisms? He could always keep using them, especially in Dublin – but somehow they didn't feel quite his.

Celine opened her purse, unfolded what appeared to be socks, and showed him two shattered pieces of glass.

'One of Maggy's swans,' she said. 'It flew off the piano. I thought maybe I'd glue it back together, but –'

'I mean, two swans stay together for life,' Luke said, 'but I'm not sure about two halves of one swan.'

'They don't always stay together. Swans divorce.'

'Really?'

'Usually from failure to breed.'

Luke couldn't help laughing. 'Ever the romantic.'

'You're the romantic. Take the swan.'

'I don't want it.'

'Can we drop it in the river?' Celine said. 'That's a nice thought, isn't it? Letting the halves bob away.'

'Nice thought,' Luke said. 'Reality is they'll slit a duck's throat.'

'I take that back about you being romantic.'

'Maybe neither of us is romantic and we need to dispose of this swan.'

They retraced their steps, since they'd seen rubbish bins

earlier along the path. 'I guess,' Celine said, 'you could argue that recycling is romantic. You'll lose everything you love, but the love comes back in another form, et cetera.'

'You can't recycle broken glass,' Luke said.

'Stop.'

'Safety reasons.'

'Fine,' Celine said. 'I'll fix the swan.'

Now they'd reached one of the park's entrance gates. They hugged, and her head folded tidily below his chin. For a moment he thought she'd look up, but her eyes stayed downcast. When they broke the embrace, she nearly dropped her bridal purse. By reflex, he grasped for it. No need. She'd caught it herself.

'Best of luck –' Luke said. He nearly said: with the swan, but he meant best of luck with everything.

'You, too,' she told him.

They said goodbye.

Acknowledgements

I'd like to thank my agent Harriet Moore and editor Lettice Franklin – collaborators or accomplices, as the case may be. I'm also grateful to the rest of the teams at W&N, Hachette Ireland, Ecco, my translation publishers, and everyone else involved in making and distributing this book.

Thank you to the readers who supported my first novel. Your generosity bought me the time to write this one.

Molte grazie to the Santa Maddalena Foundation and Beatrice for a wonderful fellowship in Tuscany. Go raibh maith agaibh freisin to everyone at the Cill Rialaig Arts Centre for a beautiful week on the Kerry coast.

As a child, I read hundreds of novels before it even occurred to me that people had written them, let alone that I could be one such person. I learned my craft from fellow authors, most of them long-dead. So thank you to fiction, my favourite thing, my thing that I somehow get to do.

About the Author

Naoise Dolan is an Irish writer born in Dublin. Her debut novel *Exciting Times* was a *Sunday Times* bestseller, widely translated, and optioned for TV. She won the 2021 Hawthornden Prize and has been shortlisted and longlisted for several other prizes, including The Women's Prize for Fiction, the Dylan Thomas Prize and The Sunday Times Young Writer of the Year Award. She lives in Berlin.